Key Manatee

Also by Robert Tacoma

Key Weird
Key Weirder
Key Witch

Key Manatee

Robert Tacoma

Mango Press
Gainesville, Florida

For information address
Mango Press
P.O. Box 141261
Gainesville, FL 32614-1261
mangopress@gmail.com

This is a work of fiction. Names, characters, places, and
incidents either are products of the author's imagination or
are used fictitiously. Any resemblance to actual events or
locales or persons, living or dead, is entirely coincidental.

For information on books by Robert Tacoma:
www.tacobob.com
mangopress@gmail.com

Front cover illustration by Eva Everything.
Cover and interior design by Merrey Design.

First U.S. edition published 2007

ISBN: 978-0-9760630-3-2

10 9 8 7 6 5 4 3 2 1

For John D.

"Write without pay until somebody offers to pay."
Mark Twain

Chapter One

Consuelo said later that maybe we should have just gotten out of there, left the body for the crabs. There would be times during the next few weeks when I would tend to agree. But if we'd just left that day, there's no telling what might have happened to Key West.

It all started out innocently enough, on yet another bright, beautiful day in the tropics. Close friend and local fishing guide Slip Hanson was at the controls of my refurbished old Wilbur cruiser as we trolled for dolphin fish in the deep blue waters off Key West. I'd just set my laptop down and leaned back in the fighting chair to enjoy the soothing murmur of the boat's engine while keeping an eye on the trolling lines off the back of the boat. Time for a moment of reflection on just how good things were going for me. Not too long a moment though, since often about the time I figured I had life by the tail, the tail grew teeth.

I've been around enough to get my share of life's less appealing surprises. Things like locusts, floods, tornados, determined but inept career criminals, and cranky law enforcement personnel. But after a quick inventory of my current situation, I knew for sure I had things right this time.

That's when I heard a sound not unlike a snore from the control deck, followed immediately by the sound a moving thirty-two-foot fishing boat makes when coming into contact with something other than water.

I jumped up for a look off the port side while a now wide-awake Slip checked the starboard. We'd run up on an offshore weedline with a big wad of branches and trash in it — the leftovers from a recent hurricane near-miss. Slip cut the engine and gave me a sheepish look and a shrug.

"Oops."

"This the spot? You said floating weedlines with trash in 'em tend to attract fish. This one seems to at least attract fishing boats."

Slip didn't really get a chance to answer. The other member of the crew, the painfully attractive Consuelo, stomped out of the galley just then and dumped something over the side. Two angry blue eyes burned from under blond page-boy hair.

"So much for the soufflé I worked on all morning! Slip, tell me you didn't fall asleep again!"

The poor fella was backed up against the bulkhead by a little over five foot of unmitigated fury wielding a formidable-looking soufflé pan. Slip gave the ship's cook a little shrug and a sorrowful look. Things were about to get ugly when line started screaming off one of the trolling reels. I came to Slip's rescue yet again.

"Call for you, Slip! Line one!"

Slip tipped his hat to the lady, "Excuse me, miss."

He leapt over to the bending rod and reel, and the fight was on. Slip commenced to alternate between grimacing and grinning.

"I think we got ourselves a big wahoo here, Taco!"

Line was coming off the reel so fast it was starting to smoke. I hoped there was enough line on the reel, since we weren't going to be chasing any fish with the boat stuck. But Slip did everything right while we yelled encouragement to the fish as well as the fisherman. Slip seemed to be making some headway when the line started peeling out again.

"Stop, you fish!"

He had his thumb on the smoking reel trying to slow the fish down. Consuelo threw her pan back in the galley and started reeling in the other line to get it clear when something hit that one too.

"I got something, but it's not very big!"

Which is when what turned out to be a nearly thirty-pound bull dolphin made his first run, and Consuelo changed her mind about what she had.

"Holy shit! It's big now!"

It took a blistered thumb, but Slip got his fish stopped and started working it back to the boat. Our petite cook was making unladylike grunting noises in the fighting chair now, working hard against her fish.

"Look in the water, TB! What are those?"

I looked over the far side where she was pointing with her elbow and saw fish in the clear blue water.

"Dolphin! Schoolies! You two stay busy, I'm on it!"

I dropped a line over with a live bait and hooked into the first of several nice school dolphin that would be find-

ing their way into our icebox that day. I had to hand it to
Slip. He'd said earlier he would put us on fish, and with
us sitting up on the tangle of sea trash, he had, literally.

The three of us were pretty well occupied working our
fish, and it wasn't until the wind shifted that I noticed
something smelled bad. I looked over at the man with the
funny hat and the seriously bent fishing rod.

"What is that gawd-awful smell, Slip?"

"Looks like a dead pelican stuck in the branches over
here on my side. That or a manatee."

Consuelo made a face.

"I thought it was Slip that smelled!"

A minute later, Consuelo gaffed her own fish and flipped
it into the icebox. She had the long-handled gaff ready again
and was leaning over the side of the boat. This gave her a
good shot at Slip's wahoo, and us a good look at some
shapely butt coming out the bottom of her cut-offs.

"You guys aren't looking at my ass are you?"

She reached back and gave herself a little pat.

"It's a toss between looking at your ass or that dead
pelican for me."

Slip was proud of that one, and Consuelo gave him the
finger once quick before snagging his wahoo and pulling
the five-foot fish with the razor-sharp teeth into the boat
in one motion. Slip was impressed.

"Nice work, Consuelo!"

My two grinning companions high-fived before getting
the big fish in the box. I had my schoolie coming to the
boat by then, and Consuelo leaned over the side next to
me with the gaff, ready.

"Let's see your fish, Taco! This sure is going to make
up for those other trips!"

No doubt. The other two trips since we'd gotten the old Wilbur cruiser fitted-out had been most notable for their lack of fish.

"I thought we talked about you wearing a bit more clothes while we're out here."

I was sounding like her father, which I surely wasn't, but with Consuelo maybe twenty-one, I was definitely old enough to be. She gave me a serious look for just a second, like she was reading me, then a wink as she gaffed my fish without taking her eyes from my face. I wish she wouldn't do things like that.

"Nice fish, Taco!"

And it was. We were some happy campers pulling in fish. All the hard work we'd put into the old boat was a distant memory as we landed several more five- to ten-pound schoolie dolphin. Consuelo bounced around the cockpit in her shorts and bikini top, gaffing fish for us like she'd been doing it all her life. I wish I hadn't said anything about her clothes, but she'd taken to having a crush on me a few weeks earlier when I'd helped her sisters find a missing friend. Since then she'd taken every opportunity to show me what was available. It was more than a little distracting at times.

It's not like there isn't a fine person inside that gorgeous body. There certainly is, but I hadn't allowed myself to be swayed by her charms for a couple of reasons. Besides the age thing, I was also already romantically involved with a woman named Mary Ann who lived in Orlando.

"Slip, I think we pretty well got our fill of fish. Should be plenty for the smoker, and I know Consuelo's sisters would be proud to take some off our hands. Maybe we should be seeing if we can get ourselves unstuck here."

"Aye, aye, Sir!"

Slip gave me a sloppy salute and cranked the engine. I stowed tackle while Consuelo washed down the deck with buckets of seawater.

"Have a seat *mi Capitán.* I'll see if I can find you a cold one."

"Thanks Consuelo, that sounds like a mighty fine idea." I eased on back into the very custom fighting chair. A barber's chair in its former life, Slip had proudly come up with it one day. He'd traded out some stone crab claws with the fella at the used furniture place in Marathon.

But before the lady who liked to refer to herself around the marina as my first mate and I could pop our Coronas, there was work to do.

"Taco, you and Julia Child here need to use those boat poles, see if you can help get us unstuck."

We were full speed reverse, and not moving. Some pushing, grunting, and cussing finally got us loose, but it also kicked up the bad smell again.

"Jesus wept, but that's bad, Slip. You say it's a bird or a manatee?"

He cut the engines back and looked over that way.

"It looks like a manatee all right, but this one's wearing shoes."

Chapter Two

The dead guy turned out to be Jessy Brown, known to all as JB, and a candidate for mayor of Key West. He was dressed up in a manatee costume. Though I didn't really know the man, I'd heard of the colorful musician turned politician. Actually, I kind of had him in mind when I came up with the Artie Mann character in my bestseller-in-progress, a coincidence I found a mite disconcerting. Though I'd been working on my book for only a few weeks, I already had almost a full page finished. Actually, I wrote that the first day, then got stuck on despair.

> The next to last time anyone saw Artie Mann alive, he was drunk and naked and had just won the Florida Lottery.
>
> A gay street mime of notorious reputation, Artie was backstage at the annual Key West Queen for a Day Pageant when he found out his weekly ticket was worth 9 million big ones. In a state of shock from his sudden

good fortune, he nearly decided to
forgo the swimsuit competition but,
after downing a celebratory bottle
of rum in record time, decided
instead to just forgo the swimsuit.

The very last time anyone saw
Artie alive was soon after sunrise
the next morning. Actually, it was
just Artie's car that was spotted by
a Cuban man netting mullet. The
fisherman looked up just in time to
see the convertible going off the
open span of a drawbridge.

Flocking from near and far the
very next day, Artie's suddenly
numerous and deeply anguished
relatives gathered to mourn the loss
of Artie. When it was learned that
all of his personal effects were
accounted for, all except the
winning lottery ticket, the despair

After delving into the depths of despair again, I finally
came up with "unfathomable despair" and called it a day.
Time for a stretch and some reflecting on the coincidences
of life.

I decided the gay, lottery-winning character of my
book didn't really have much in common with the contro-
versial mayoral candidate other than both owned convert-
ibles, both drank a lot of rum, and both were very much
mysteriously disappeared. That is, until we made our
grisly discovery offshore.

"Man oh man, Taco, that sure was a grisly discovery we made yesterday."

The floor of my living room moved as Slip paced and I relaxed on my worn, yet comfortable yellow couch. I wondered about the movement and took a look out the window. A big cruiser coming into the marina had just come by my old houseboat, *Sandy Bottomed Girl,* a little too close and a little too fast. Slip was acting as anxious as a long-tailed cat in a room full of rocking chairs. He kept eyeing the phone on the wall.

"Mind if I use the phone?"

"Make it quick in case the police or Coast Guard want to call again with the same questions they spent three hours asking us out on the water yesterday." I gave the man a look. "And be careful."

Slip's the only person I know can misdial calling pizza delivery and get the governor's wife's cell phone instead. But that would be about par for the course for Slip. Man always seemed to have about the worse luck any fella could have with anything mechanical. As good a friend as he's been since we met at the marina, I got to admit, part of being around the man is seeing what life's going to throw at him next. Not that I was hurting for excitement. Since I'd been in Key West, it seemed like there was always something about to land in my lap when I least expected it.

It was still early morning, and I'd been up late the night before, so when Slip took the phone up front I must have started nodding. I noticed a weight in my lap that quickly turned into a full-sized girl, complete with purring sounds and soft whispers.

"Mmmm. Taco, you look so peaceful when you're asleep."

Normally, I'm a bit more aware and harder to sneak up on, and it bothered me that Consuelo was able to plant her shapely self on me so easily. It also bothered me that I wasn't getting as upset as I should have.

"Miss, could you kindly extricate yourself from my personal space here?" This got me a frown. "And anyway, I wasn't asleep. I was just resting my eyes."

"Uh-huh. You know who you remind me of? That movie guy, Clint Eastwood."

I tried to give my lap ornament a shove and a quick whack on the rear, but she was on her feet and across the room before I could get in a swing. There was a small book of crossword puzzles in my lap, one I hadn't seen before.

"Where'd you get this?"

I'd been hooked on the sometimes aggravating, but decidedly vocabulary enhancing, puzzles since my days of possum ranching in Texas. She looked up from inspecting one of the small statues I had on a top shelf in the lounge and gave a slow wink.

"I'm a very resourceful person, sir. In case you hadn't noticed." She put the idol back on the shelf with the others. "I've been meaning to ask you about these, is this gold? Sure looks like gold."

I said someone had told me they were called Chac-mools, but before I could launch into that particular story, Slip slipped inside to put the phone back.

"Hey, Taco, I got a — ." He noticed the idol inspector across the room and gave her a sideways look, "Oh, hey, Blondie. How's tricks?"

"You got a what, Slip? Some secret you can't tell the little girly about? Big shipment of penile implants you ordered for yourself on the Internet?"

By the way Slip was bowing up I could tell where this was going.

"Could you two kindly take your cat fight out on the aft deck? Makes for less mess if I have to use a bucket of water to break it up." They both stomped toward the door as I went back to my new book.

"And thanks for the crosswords, Consuelo." She lost the fire in her eyes long enough to give me a quick wink just as the phone rang. Slip turned at the door, but his feuding partner hopped across the room like a gazelle.

"Captain Bob's residence, First Mate Consuelo speaking!" A couple seconds later Consuelo made a terrible face and held the phone like it had turned into a dead rat. "It's — her."

I caught the tossed phone with Consuelo making gagging sounds on her way out to join Slip.

Mary Ann, calling from her place in Orlando, was none too happy about Consuelo answering the phone. It took a while to smooth things over before the love of my life got around to breaking the news — she had to help train someone new at work over the weekend. So much for our highly anticipated romantic rendezvous at the Hungry Mullet Bed and Breakfast in Key Largo. I tried to hide my disappointment as best I could while we talked about the lack of updates from the authorities on the grisly discovery. After a little more catching up, it was decided we'd get together the following weekend come hell or high water.

After we said our goodbyes, I put the phone back on the wall and got comfortable again on the trusty old yellow couch. I could see my fishing partners out on the deck were still in the name-calling and threatening stage, squared off like they were about to tear into one another. Slip was tall and thin like me and about the same age, but a hard life on the water made him look older. He also looked tough as nails, which he was. His snarling opponent, crouched and circling while dispatching an impressive stream of profanity, looked like your basic fresh-faced college co-ed, which she wasn't.

To the handful of tourists watching from a safe distance onshore at the marina, it must have looked like a pretty uneven fight about to go down, and it would be. I don't doubt Slip would punch a girl out if he had to, but there were stories about the fighting abilities of this particular young lady. I couldn't imagine he'd be foolish enough to let things come to blows. Especially since he was the one told me the stories.

A good head taller, Slip bobbed and weaved in a classic boxing stance while Consuelo circled low, moving her clawed hands around like she was picking cotton, or disemboweling somebody. Her hands didn't fit the rest of her. They were calloused and scarred.

"Come on! Come on, Slip, you know you want to hit me! You know you want to hit the little girly!"

Those two looked so fierce, I almost didn't notice the cop car pull up beside my old pickup truck in the parking lot. I peeled myself from the couch for a breath of fresh air on the aft deck.

The big lawman came up to the gawking tourists who had gathered to watch the fight, stopped, and looked over the situation. He gave his cop belt a quick adjustment then looked at the confused tourists again.

"What's going on here? What you people looking at?" He next looked toward my cohorts.

Slip and Consuelo had already seen him and were locked up together cheek to cheek, humming loud, and doing what looked like a passable dance step. They stopped in mid-stride and gave the officer big, innocent smiles. Slip nodded toward the policeman.

"Polka. Just learning the little lady here some fancy footwork, officer." Then, self-conscious smiles before returning to their lessons, humming what sounded like show tunes. The large, burly instrument of the law turned his attention high-beams on me.

"Looking for a Taco Bob, supposed to live on this houseboat. That you?"

"He just left, headed over to Sloppy Joe's. Jimmy Buffett's in town, supposed to be playing there in about an hour. We might get him on his cell phone though."

The cop came up the dock to the back of my houseboat and took note of the sudden lack of gawking tourists. He gave up a smile.

"Works on 'em every time."

"That it does, officer. I'm Taco Bob, what can I do for you?"

"Just need to take a quick look inside. Got an anonymous call there was a meth lab on your boat."

"That so? Last week it was a pot farm, week before it was hiding runaways. Any idea who's making those calls?"

"We're pretty sure it's the same person. Cell phone with a scrambled number." He gave me a shrug. "I still need to take a look inside though, if you don't mind."

Slip and his dancing partner were close enough to hear. We three looked over at the luxurious houseboat three boats down and saw the corner of a window curtain move quick.

I gave the lawman the nickel tour. Showed him the master stateroom with the oversized bed, the spacious bath, guest quarters, lounge, and full galley. One of the storage places I showed him had a collection of women's clothes that had come with the boat.

"Sure is a nice old houseboat you got here. Thanks for showing me around."

By the time he left, my fishing partners were gone too. Before I could get into thinking about somebody trying to put the cops on me again, Slip was back, looking anxious.

"Taco, I need to borrow a big wrench. None of mine are big enough."

"Help yourself, just don't forget where it came from." He headed for the tool locker. "Don't suppose I could ask what a fishing guide who only has a kayak with no motor needs a big wrench for?"

"Oh, it's not for anything of mine. I'm helping Capt. Roy work on his new boat." He came back with my biggest crescent wrench. "Well, not exactly helping him. He's off at the store or something, so I thought I'd get started on the engine while I was waiting for him to get back."

"Uh, Slip. Not that it's my place to say, but given your track record with mechanical things, you might want to let Capt. Roy be around before you do anything. In fact —"

The phone rang and Slip was gone.

I watched him scoot across the marina while finding out from the phone what it was he started to tell me earlier. The caller was Trisha Everything, an acquaintance of Slip's and owner of one of Key West's more popular restaurants, the Blue Parrot just off Duval Street. She was having a problem and said one word that did it for me, but she didn't want to talk about it further on the phone. Wanted to know if I could stop by later. About then Slip was back, even more anxious.

"Hey, Taco. That Ms. Everything? Yeah, I meant to tell you she wants to meet with you. Real top secret stuff of some kind." He was talking fast. "I just need to borrow your fire extinguisher, the big one." And he was off again.

I told the lady I'd be by in a little while. Just as I hung the phone up, it rang. I was told by a recording not to hang up, I may have won something important. So I hung up and it rang again. Coast Guard wanted to go over a few gruesome details.

Just as they were winding down, Capt Roy stuck his head in the door. He had a look in his eye.

"You seen Slip?" Man sure had a loud voice.

"Thought he was helping you?"

I got the look again and some grumbling. Capt. Roy stomped back down the dock, and I went back to answering the same questions again for the Coast Guard. Just as I hung up, Consuelo walked in.

"Consuelo, I got a meet in town. You can hang here if you want, just lock up when you leave." The phone rang as I headed out.

"Captain Bob's residence, First Mate Consuelo speaking!"

She held the phone away from her ear and made a bad face letting me know I was in trouble again. I sighed and reached for the phone.

"Gotcha! Not her!" She put a hand over the phone. "You go about your business, I'll field this one for you." She checked her watch and gave a quick wave. I could hear her as I closed the door. "Why yes, I'd love to hear about four nights and three days in beautiful Orlando!"

Before I could think about Consuelo keeping the poor telemarketer on the phone long enough to beat Slip's record, I noticed Capt. Roy walking deliberately through the parking lot carrying a large fish gaff.

"You seen him?"

Actually, I did, behind the captain on the other side of some cars. Slip was waving his hands and shaking his head. I held my hands palm up and shrugged on my way to the truck. I didn't have time for these fellas' foolishness. I had a meeting about voodoo.

Chapter Three

The Blue Parrot doesn't usually have any live parrots, but they always got plenty of live chickens. The infamous wild chickens that run the streets of Key West had long ago taken a liking to the outdoor dining area of the popular restaurant.

I had a seat at a table outside with Trisha Everything, a trim, round-faced young lady with a tiny nose and eyes that always seemed to be wide open. This topped with a big mop of hair the same bright blue as her eyes made her quite a sight. Since taking over the restaurant a couple years earlier, she'd earned herself a reputation among the locals for being eccentric, if not downright crazy. No small accomplishment in a place like Key West.

We sat in the shade, enjoying a cool drink and the breeze rustling the palm fronds overhead while mouth-watering cooking smells drifted over from the kitchen. There were chickens around our feet and a dog barking on the other side of the wood fence.

"It's not like I'm short on the sodding birds, and the bloody tourists love them." She gave a quick kick under the table at a scrawny hen, which jumped five feet and issued some angry cackling. "But the way they been turning up dead, I'm telling you, finding a dead chicken by the door nearly every morning is a mite unnerving." The neighbor dog had it down to a steady deep bark now. "And shut your flipping mouth, you!"

"So you think it's voodoo, the dead chicken on the doorstep?" She gave me an incredulous look.

"What bloody else could it be? My cook, Freddy, said he saw some flick once had that sort of thing. I just don't want my waitresses and cooks quitting, afraid they'll be next on the stoop."

This all made a small amount of sense to me, not that I was any expert on voodoo. But along with all the other wild tales floating around Key West, there were a few involving voodoo.

"You don't suppose somebody's doing that just to scare you? Anybody got a reason to do your business some harm? Any enemies in town?"

This got her thinking. I would ask about former boyfriends, but I had it on good authority she didn't do much dating, too busy with the restaurant. That and her way of talking. It wasn't the hair or British slang keeping the men away. It was what she held in her hand when she talked. I decided to try the boyfriends anyway.

"Any former boyfriends might be up to something crazy like this?"

"Ha, as if! What boyfriends? Geezers in this town think a girl strange just because she talks with a doll!" I knew I shouldn't have mentioned the boyfriend thing. "Right dodgy arseholes, the lot of them!"

It was a bit weird, talking to a vibrant, healthy, blue-haired young woman who never moved her lips and held up a worn-looking little ceramic doll like it was the one actually talking.

"Miss Everything, — "

"Steady on, call me Trish. It's my name."

"Okay, Trish. I'm not going to make any promises here, but I'll do some checking around, see what I can find out from my sources."

"Slip, he told me once you knew about mysticism and that lot."

"He told you that, did he? Well, I don't really —"

Trish leaned forward and held the doll closer.

"Slip said you were a dreamer." Before I could say anything, she put her free hand on mine. For some reason I was surprised it was so soft. "No matter. I will see you right if you get this sodding voodoo from my caf."

I looked at Trish and talked arrangements with a five-inch doll for a few minutes. Since I didn't feel right taking her money, we agreed I'd be paid for my time in free meals for myself and friends. A cook came out and handed his boss a phone.

"It's the new Marty, Ms. Jeager. Says he can't make it." It wasn't until Trish took the phone that I realized she'd had her hand on mine still. She held the phone against her chest so the doll could whisper to me.

"Bloody hell! That JB played here the first weekend every month, now I can't find a bloody soul to replace him. He only got himself dead, you know." I indicated I'd heard something to that effect.

Folks born in Key West are usually called conchs. Those born somewhere else but living in town for enough years are know as freshwater conchs. Having lived in Key West for over ten years, JB easily qualified as a freshwater conch. He'd been one of several musicians doing Marty Manatee impersonation gigs in the bars, restaurants, and street corners of Key West. These days the original Marty is a living legend after getting his start singing ballads in Key West bars back in the '70s. But while most of the singing manatees went for the traditional tropics music, JB tended to go more for the blues.

I told Ms. Everything I'd get back to her soon, then excused myself so we could both get to work. While she went about trying to locate a new singing manatee, I went to see what I could find out about voodoo.

I started my search with the one person I knew who had a line on almost everyone on the island — Slip Hanson. I found him having lunch a couple rows over from the *Sandy Bottomed Girl*. His host was Jimmy Redd, the most envied man in Key West and owner of a pretty little sailboat named the *Herring*. They were sitting in the cockpit, working on a plate of fried fish and a six-pack. Jimmy looked happy, as always. His long, sandy hair and boyish good looks made for a combination the ladies found hard to resist.

"Hey, Taco! Come on aboard and have a grouper nugget!" He handed me a couple of nice-looking pieces of fish on a paper plate and tossed a smaller piece in the air toward Slip. Slip pulled a beer can away from his face just in time to snap the fish nugget out of the air. He killed the beer and belched a thanks as I sat down. I thought the fish was excellent.

"Mighty fine, Jimmy! Cornmeal breading?"

"Corn base with my secret spices. Caught the grouper this morning fishing for grunts right here under the boat."

"Reckon that was a surprise." I finished off the fish and took a good pull on the offered beer.

"Care for more?"

I politely waved off the almost empty platter my host held up. Slip was up for more though and let loose a couple of near-perfect dog barks. This along with the begging position and the sad eyes thing earned him another tossed morsel. I've seen variations of this work for the man in situations involving women as well. I needed to talk to Slip.

"If I could interrupt y'all practicing for the Mallory Square Follies for just a minute, I need to ask Rover here what he knows about voodoo."

That got their attention. Slip gave me a squint-eye look.

"This got anything to do with that favor you were going to check on?"

"As a matter of fact. Thought you might know somebody in town I could ask a few questions doing with animal sacrifices and such."

Slip went to rubbing his chin and squinting at me, Jimmy, and the rest of the fish nuggets.

"Might ask ol' Mama Rosa the palm reader, or better yet, Levita the Voodoo Priestess. She has that place on Fleming a couple blocks off Duval." Slip ate another fish nugget to help himself think. "Her place is on Fleming, ain't it, Jimbo?"

Jimmy Redd hadn't said a word or even twitched since I mentioned voodoo.

"Uh, yeah, Slip. Near the bookstore, I think."

Man looked like he'd seen a ghost. Slip took advantage of our host's wandering concentration and scooped the last of the fish morsels into his shirt pocket as he stood up.

"I reckon I better go along with Taco Bob here, make sure he don't get lost." He gave the man who lived a charmed life a thumbs-up and wink combo. "Thanks again for the snack."

Slip bailed on me before we even got out of the marina. He saw Capt. Roy loping along toward the marina office.

"I just thought of some stuff I'm needing from the store." And was gone around the corner before I could say anything.

I headed on over to where I keep my trusty old bicycle and seen the owner of the fancy houseboat. A big man with Donald Trump hair, he was standing on the dock with his considerable gut pulled in talking to a couple of young tourist women. I smiled as I walked by.

He ignored me, but the women gave up shy smiles when I tipped my hat. The man gestured toward his boat, bragging some unlikely tale about winning it in a card game. I'd just about got to my bike when I heard a loud slap. The big guy had a hand to the red mark on his face. He started in yelling angry words at the two women as they stomped away on down the dock.

I rode Ol' Rusty along the side streets, doing my best to avoid any sudden mergers with the numerous scooters, cars, and tour buses on the fast track to paradise. Parking places in Old Town are scarce as hen's teeth, and drivers are usually more focused on looking for parking than actually driving. You ride a bike in Key West very much, you tend to get eyes in the back of your head.

I turned down Fleming and kept an eye peeled. Just before Island Books, a small sign pointed down an alley and offered Death Charms, Voodoo Supplies, and Scooter Rentals.

I locked Rusty to a post and walked by a row of shiny scooters in the narrow alley. A crow sitting on one of the scooters squawked a good one before flying off. A side door in the old wooden building opened to a poorly lit room of masks and costumes, jewelry and charms, trinkets and oddities. One of the oddest things in the room was the old black woman behind the counter. As my eyes adjusted to the light, I noticed she appeared to have snakes in her hair.

"What's your pleasure, sailor?"

"Howdy, ma'am. Nice place."

She gave me a sleepy look with bloodshot eyes as she tried to figure me out.

"You don't look like a man be wanting no scooter."

"No, ma'am."

"Maybe you looking for licensed hypnotist? I got license." She shoved what appeared to be an expired driver's license in my face.

"Actually, I was hoping I could ask you a couple questions." That got her going on a short burst of cackling laughter.

"You a man with a problem, no?"

The old gal leaned forward on her stool and made a sweep with her hand over the things in the glass case between us. The snakes turned out to be colored beads over braids of hair with eyes on the bottom beads and hair strands out the end like a snake's forked tongue.

"Perhaps I could interest you in one of these here genuine gold amulets? Got a fine selection guaranteed to bring love, money, health, or revenge. You needing a spell to take care of a rival, perhaps?" She made a gesture to signify male private parts with one hand and scissors with the other. "Maybe something in a gold or silver good luck charm? Or if you on a budget, this fine charm here perfect then! Work every time, no doubt!" She reached down and came up with a rather tired-looking rabbit's foot to dangle in my face.

"Well, no. Actually I just —"

"Ah! I know what you looking for! You come to a voodoo shop, you want the real thing, no? Look down here at these on the bottom. Smart man like you wants a direct line to spirit! Our All-Purpose Voodoo Doll very popular with men. Fix you up for all kinds of women problems, and what man don't have women problems? We just get new shipment in from Haiti." She stuck a small doll that looked like it was made from rolls of yarn in my face. "You buy one of these, I guarantee you get wood like teenager, money come to you in mail, and boss man get the loose bowels every time he yell at you!"

She kept the doll in my face and lit up a grin to show off years of dental neglect.

"Actually, I just wanted to ask —"

"Answer questions free. Doll fifteen ninety-nine!"

I got the hint and handed her a twenty, which immediately disappeared. I got the doll and an eyebrow raised in query. It didn't look like I was getting any change.

"I wanted to ask about sacrifices, like with chickens." This got me a narrow-eyed look of deep thought and a slow head shake. "Somebody I know's been finding dead chickens on their doorstep and I told 'em I'd ask around. I thought maybe someone of your obvious expertise in voodoo might put me on the right track."

As she gave this a good mulling over, the first few notes of the theme song from *The Exorcist* came from behind the counter. She pulled out a cellphone and checked the number before turning away from me to take the call.

"Newspaperman, that you?"

I took the opportunity to check out the rest of the store. There really wasn't much merchandise besides some dusty masks and costumes on the walls and the stuff in the big glass counter. A shelf by the door had some scooter accessories and a box marked "Shrunken Heads." While I contemplated taking a peek in the box, the voodoo lady was giving someone hell.

"I tell you, mister, that island is cursed! Long ago, old voodoo witch and friends live there until giant monster with thousand eyes come from the sea one night! Eyes glow in dark and all people except voodoo witch scared and leave! Then baby monster come from mother and white devils jump on island. What? Yes, called cruise ship now."

While avoiding the box, I noticed some photos on the back wall. Most were of a younger version of the old woman standing with various local people and some celebrities. The newest photo was of JB in his Marty Manatee outfit standing alone in front of Capt. Tony's Bar. There were several big pins sticking in the photo.

"White devils show voodoo witch papers and say she has to leave island so devils can build castles for more devils called Yank Keys. Witch mad and put spell on island. Big hurricane come, flood island — kill witch and devils all. Now these many years later, they want to bring deserted island to Key West, but I tell you this — That island is still cursed!"

I wandered back over toward the box.

"Yes, mister newspaperman, that whole damn story. … Yes, all true. It happen long time ago. … Huh? Cash, no check. … Paypal? Okay, but make it soon! I have to go to post office this afternoon, check if big shipment of pins and dolls look like newspaper men come in yet. … Fine then, pleasure doing business with you."

I just opened the box for a peek and immediately wished I hadn't.

"All first-class genuine stuff! Fifty-nine ninety-nine each, or two for a hundred. You know what they say about two heads!"

"Thanks, but I'll pass." She gave me a shrug and a look like I was missing out on one of the world's greatest bargains.

"Uh, about the chicken sacrifices?"

"Oh, yeah. Let me think on this."

She went back to mulling, then looked up and smiled way too big. I took an involuntary half-step toward the door.

"I know man you need to talk to! Know all kind of low-lifes do these kinds of things! Must be most evil man in Key West! Real bastard, him!" She looked around the room carefully, then motioned me closer so she could whisper. "Evil old man called Shark Hunter. You go see him at the Scorpion Pit Bar." She reached under the counter and handed me another doll, this one black and red. "He ask you who send you, just give him this!"

She sat back on her stool and launched into cackling and coughing. As the door closed behind me, I thought I heard the old woman giggle like a little girl.

Chapter Four

"How about Floaters restaurant? They got good, cheap stone crabs."

"It sank."

"Again? Hmmm. Governor's is close, and I haven't been there in a while."

"I heard since he opened his third place, he's so busy he's gone to using real chicken."

"What did he use before?"

"Don't ask."

"Well, it can't be much worse than some of the stuff we used to eat on the possum ranch back in Texas. The governor, he gave me a ride once, you know."

I think I seen Slip roll his eyes as we headed out the door to go eat. I guess I may have already told that story a time or two.

Slip ordered the Workingman's Bean Surprise and I got the Chicken Burritos. When the food came, we didn't hesitate and got to it.

We'd both done some serious initial damage to our entrées before doing any talking. Though no slouch when it comes to putting away groceries, I tend to savor my food more than Slip. I seen him eyeing my last burrito as he was licking out the bowl his beans had come in.

"The answer is yes, I'm going to eat that. The other answer is also yes, it tastes like chicken."

Slip pushed back in his chair and produced a big toothpick and went to work, still giving my burrito an occasional covetous glance.

"I don't want it, Taco. I reckon I got enough surprises for one meal with the beans already. No telling about that burrito, been a lot of traffic on the highway lately, if you know what I mean." I used my elbow to slide the burrito back out of temptations way. "Did you find the Voodoo Priestess?"

"Yep. She told me to check with a man called Shark Hunter." The toothpick fell out of Slip's mouth, but he didn't move or say anything. "Thought I'd look him up later today."

Slip didn't move, just swallowed hard.

"I'd love to tag along, but I got a charter this afternoon. Big-time flyfisher out of Maine wants to see some bonefish."

Slip had a good thing going taking folks out kayak-fishing the backwaters. The kayak wasn't the man's first choice in marine transportation, but his long-standing tradition of mechanical ineptitude with any sort of engine left him with few options.

"I reckon I'll be heading over to the Scorpion Pit by myself then."

"Best to go there early. That's a mighty rough place at night, TB." The man surprised me with a rare serious look. "I'm liable to be late with this charter. You go there after dark, you might want to take Consuelo."

"I'm not about to take a girl to a place like that, Slip. I can't believe you'd even say such a thing." I polished off the last burrito, threw some bills on the table and headed for the door. Slip was still with the weird serious stuff.

"Taco, she ain't what you think."

Fish Daddy is one of those Key West folks you rarely come across outside of a barroom. But just a few days earlier, I'd seen a familiar bright green parrot bopping along above the heads of the tourists on Duval Street. Upon closer inspection I could see the bird perched on a hat worn by none other than Fish himself, out in broad daylight. He was navigating one of those coolers on wheels down the sidewalk at a good clip when he saw me across the street.

"Taco! Hold on, partner! I got something for you!" Without looking, he made a beeline across Duval and a screaming tourist girl on a rental motorbike just missed the cooler — the bird screeching and holding on for all he was worth. Fish Daddy didn't pay the close call any mind and was all smiles, shaking my hand.

"I got some fresh-caught grouper here you can smoke up for some of your famous smoked-fish spread!"

Before I could say anything, the man pushed two big bags of fish fillets into my chest then scurried off down the street.

So several days later on my way to try to find Shark Hunter, I stopped by Pirate Jim's Bar and Grill to drop off

Fish Daddy's big bowl of smoked-fish spread. Which meant I had plenty for myself too, since my fee for making the savory pâté is half. The man sat at his usual place at the bar.

"Taco! You got the stuff?" He opened the paper bag with the spread and stuck his nose in for a good snort. "Man, oh, man, but that smells fine!" He waved the barmaid over, and she came up with a box of Stoned Wheat crackers from under the bar. The old man pulled a giant folding knife out of his shorts and, after slicing open the cracker box, went to lathering up crackers with the spread. He gave the bird a cracker to keep him quiet. I declined the offer of a top-heavy cracker, and so did the barmaid. The knife looked suspiciously similar to the one he used to trim his toenails most nights while sitting at the bar.

"Y'all don't know what you're missing!" He went to eating and mumbling his approval of the spread, then started loading up another cracker. "How's that book you're writing coming along?"

"How'd you hear about that?"

"Oh, hell, most of the town knows." I got a little jab in the ribs with an elbow. "You go around asking folks about writing, and it ain't hard to figure out why."

"Well, I've got a start on a book."

"Good for you! I'm going to write one myself if I ever get the time." Which I imagine would be whenever he gets caught up on hanging out in bars and chasing women. "I got some advice for you on your book. Don't forget to throw in some supernatural stuff. Folks really eat that crap up."

"Thanks, I'll keep it in mind." I wanted to get on over to the Scorpion Pit and was about to take the opportunity.

"Before you rush off, Taco, I got a lucid dreaming story for you. As you know, there ain't all that many folks into lucid dreaming, so I was mighty surprised when this fella starts in telling me this weird story."

I sat back down. A draft beer appeared on the bar in front of me. I took a long sip.

"Said he'd been trying for months to dream lucid but just couldn't seem to get the hang of it. He'd read all the books and even bought some of those subliminal tapes and CDs. Nothing. Couldn't wake up in his dreams. But he kept at it and then got hold of one of those mask things supposed to help you dream lucid?"

I gave a nod that I'd heard of such a thing.

"Anyway, first time he tries it he not only goes lucid, he comes up on a dreaming scout!"

From what I'd heard, nobody was quite sure just what a scout was, except they seemed to be a lot more real than anything else you're likely to come up on in lucid dreaming. Some thought you could ask the scouts questions, though few trusted the answers. The old man was really getting into it.

"So what does he do, you ask? Well, he told me old Charlie Spider said in his book you're supposed to grab hold any scouts you see and hang on tight, so he did!" A quick break for a spread and cracker and a gulp of beer and he was back. "Said the scout started spinning like crazy, trying to throw him off but he held on. Said he spun for days."

The man went for more beer and his attention strayed when he noticed the barmaid bending over to pick something up. I wanted to hear the rest of the story.

"So what happened next? After he was spinning around?"

"That's it. He said when he stopped spinning, he found himself in a bar talking to a fella with a green parrot on his head." A finger pointed toward the restroom. "That's him now, the dazed-looking fella coming out of the facilities."

I stood up to give the dreamer his seat back and headed out the door to find Shark Hunter.

Chapter Five

I knew about the Scorpion Pit Bar, but I'd never been there. There's plenty of stories about the place, and every so often something in the paper about the health department closing it down.

The bar's in an old fish house down by the shrimp docks, not far from Jimmy Buffett's secret recording studio. Regulars sit up on the roof deck to watch the boats and drink. There's an intersection of narrow channels close by that prove tricky for pleasure boaters in the best of conditions. Add fog, rain, weekend traffic, alcohol, testosterone, inexperienced boaters, missing channel markers, or any combination thereof, and you're likely to get some spectacular boat wrecks. I'd heard some locals call it Key West's answer to Nascar.

I finally found the place. An old concrete block building baking in the tropical sun behind some overgrown bougainvillea bushes. The faded sign on the door said Welcome to the Scorpion Pit. The door was locked. I gave it a couple good tries and was about to give up when an old fella came blinking in the sunlight from around the side of the building. He stopped, gave me the eye and seemed to come to a decision.

"Around back." He pointed with a thumb over his shoulder as he headed for the parking lot. Guess that's how they keep the tourists thinned out.

I stood inside the door for a half-minute to let my eyes adjust. A nervous young bartender wiped at the bar, and the handful of locals couldn't be bothered to glance up from their business. Except for a rough-looking couple down at the end of the bar who grinned piano teeth at me and gave quick girly-like waves and winks before going back to their private whisperings.

"What'll you have, mister?"

"I reckon I could handle a draft. Looking for Shark Hunter."

The young fella behind the bar jumped a little at the name. His hands were shaking as he set my beer on the bar. "Buck fifty. He ain't here."

"Know where I might find him?" The bartender took my money and shrugged without looking up, then beat a hasty retreat down to the other end of the bar. That's when I seen Robert looking at me from a table in the corner. It's not that I don't like Robert, but the guy can be a mite depressing to be around.

"Hey, Taco Bob! Who you looking for? Shark Hunter?"

I carried my beer down toward Robert, hoping for once I could just get a straight answer from the man.

"Yep, that's who I'm looking for. You know where he's at?"

Robert stuck a smoke in his mouth and, after a few tries, got a cigarette lighter shaped like a fishing lure to light. He took a big puff and motioned for me to have a seat. Sitting would just encourage him.

"Thanks, but I'm in a mighty big hurry to find the man." Robert didn't seem to hear me or notice me still standing and checking my watch. He just settled back in his chair, took another hit on his cigarette, and got a far-away look going.

"You know, I wanted to have a character in my next book like Shark Hunter." So much for a straight answer. "Did I ever tell you what happened? How I got screwed over by the big publishing houses?"

"As a matter of fact, you did tell me about that. At length." But it was too late, he was into it.

"Those bastards were too busy giving fat publishing contracts to authors writing the same book over and over. Too busy to pay any attention to someone trying to do something a little different." The most-avoided failed writer in Key West took a slow pull on his beer. "Taco, did I tell you I wrote and published three books all by myself? Didn't even have professional editing or anything. Just some help from friends." I hoped I could find out where Shark Hunter was before he got all emotional and started crying in his beer.

"Taco, you know, I, I could have been a contender!" Too late, tears were streaming down his cheeks.

"Robert, pull yourself together, man. I'm sure something will work out for you." I hated to lie to the man. "Maybe some big publisher will read one of your books and give you a call." I realized too late that was the wrong thing to say. Now he was really falling apart.

The locals at the other tables didn't pay any attention to the grown man crying like a baby. They'd obviously seen it before. The rough couple at the end of the bar looked over though and both winked. The strangely familiar one with the unsettling dark eyes licked her lips and blew a kiss before turning back around.

"Robert. Look, I feel for you, man, but I really need to talk to Shark Hunter if you know where he is."

After some further sniffling, the man pulled out a handkerchief and honked into it.

"He probably went to his boat. It's over at that abandoned marina they're going to tear down for condos. You know where I mean?"

"Yeah, just across the bridge. This end of Stock Island." I waved at the bartender and pointed at Robert. "Thanks for your help, partner. Let me buy you a beer."

"You're a good man, Taco Bob. You want some free advice? You ever write a book, use a lot of adjectives, the bigger the better. That's what a lot of those big-time writers do, and they've all got publishing contracts!"

Robert looked about to lose it again, so I gave him a slap on the back and told him I'd be seeing him. I handed the bartender some money and was heading for the door when Robert yelled out to me.

"Mr. Hunter's real name isn't Shark, you know. It's Clarence."

Chapter Six

I pushed open the old chain-link gate with the big Posted No Trespassing sign and drove down the pot-holed shell road. The only place I could see to park was next to a rusty hulk on blocks that looked as though it might have been a boat at one time.

The old marina had been abandoned for quite a while. The only signs of life among the collapsing buildings, underbrush, and trash were a feral cat or two and loud rock-and-roll music coming from the direction of the water. Sounded like one of Marty Manatee's big hits.

I followed a path through chest-high weeds and stands of scrubby trees until I came to a one-plank-wide walkway that went out to the source of the music — a big, squat thing in the water that looked like a cross between an old shrimp boat and a bad car wreck. Someone had welded, wired, and duct-taped a tuna tower onto the roof of the cabin and had gotten it almost straight. Several tattered nautical flags and what appeared to be equally shredded ladies' undergarments flapped from the rigging.

The plank had a little spring to it, enough so I had to pay attention or I'd be taking a swim. Before I got far, I noticed a powerful bad smell.

"Hello on board! Anybody home?" There wasn't any answer and I didn't look up from the plank until I was almost to the boat. A man sitting on deck reached down to a boombox and the music stopped. He set his book down, stood, and stretched out like he'd been sitting a while. He was a lean and rugged-looking sort, wearing an equally rugged-looking old yachting cap. The man before me was gray fuzz and dark sunglasses on top, bones and grizzle everywhere else. He was tanned almost black and naked as a newborn. I'd never seen so many scars on a human being.

"Howdy. You must be Mr. Hunter. I —"

"Hold on just a cotton-fucking minute! Before you get started on God knows whatever it is you come here for, you look sober enough to make it back to the store to buy a round." He pushed an empty gallon jug across the table by his chair and drank off the dregs of another before handing it over as well. "You can get a couple of these and something for yourself."

I gathered up the glass jugs while he gave me detailed directions to the store. The old fella issued an uninhibited belch and went back to the book he was reading. Looked like I had the honor of paying for the beer.

I drove through a weathered old trailer park I hadn't seen before and down a road that hadn't ever been troubled by paving or much traffic. Most of the area was overgrown and fenced off with government signs, except for an old clapboard house with a hand-painted sign that said "STORE." The store backed up to some low mangrove grow-

ing out in the shallow water and a bridge in the distance
jammed with traffic. Nothing else around except a tired-
looking old Pinto parked on the edge of the dusty road.

The inside was one stifling room with a couple of
chickens scratching around. The chickens spooked when
I came in knocking on the doorjamb, and a short, bald
man came snorting awake from a couch in the middle of
the room. I held the jugs up and he stood zipping his
pants as a skin magazine dropped to the floor. He didn't
say anything and didn't take his hooded eyes off me while
he headed for the bank of moldy old refrigerators along
the far wall. I set the jugs on the dusty counter he pointed
at. Without looking away from me, the wary man poured
both full from a five-gallon bucket of God-knows-what
while a fly walked across his face.

"That'll be fifteen dollars, mister!"

I pointed to some cans of beer in the open fridge.

"One of those."

He seemed unsure of the math, so I offered him a ten
and two fives. The man held the money up and counted
slowly, giving me a good show of grimy hands and black
fingernails. He kept giving me suspicious glances while
checking the bills, like he must get a lot of big-time coun-
terfeiters passing through.

The first notes of the soundtrack from *Deliverance*
came from the couch. As he answered the cellphone, I
heard some banging coming from the backyard.

"Yeah, them boys are here now. I want my money like
you promised!" The man wiped his nose with his hand
and pulled some crumpled bills from his pocket.

I decided to bail on the change and beat a hasty
retreat. I put the can of beer in my pocket and carried a

jug in each hand. I took a peek out back before I left and seen two men working out of a blue pickup, putting up a big sign facing the highway bridge. Looked like a political sign, and a perfect place for it.

When I got back to the boat, my host was in his chair reading and had thankfully pulled on a stained pair of baggy shorts he likely donned for social occasions. I noticed the smell was even stronger and seemed to come from a large pile of fur clumps and mud on the deck next to the table. The fur clumps started a low growl, which caused a cloud of low circling flies to fan out.

"Don't mind ol' Queequeg there, he ain't bit nobody in days. Ain't that right, boy?" The dog started wagging his tail, further scattering the flies. Dog was one of those breeds that's all head and teeth. Looked more like a short-tailed alligator with fur.

"Nice dog. That is a dog, right?"

"African Dung Dog. Cross between a dog and a hyena." He gave the dog a loving pat, then opened one of the jugs of booze and drank off a couple inches. He set the bottle down while shaking his head in short, violent bursts like he was trying to shake a spider off his nose. Then he went into a mild sneezing fit before lighting up a big smile. "That fella sure can brew up some fine stuff! You ought to try it sometime."

He went back to his book and seemed to forget me. I wiped my can of beer off real good before opening it, then leaned against the gunnels upwind from the dog.

"Mr. Hunter, I —"

"Reach that line behind you there going up on that piling!" He was on his feet heading for the pilothouse.

"This one?"

He didn't look.

"Yeah. Cast it off!"

I did, just as he hit the key, the motor exploded into life, and we were moving and leaving a trail of black smoke from the engine exhaust. The dog disappeared into the cabin as I came over to the pilothouse doorway. The man looked back at me and flipped up his sunglasses. He had the usual raccoon look from wearing sunglasses all the time and some unusual eyes. One unblinking eye stared straight at me while the other gave me a good looking over, head to toe. The sunglasses were the kind you see baseball outfielders wear. I was glad when he flipped them back down.

"You come here to see about making a movie about the famous Shark Hunter?"

He was still looking me over. I was about to say something about steering, when the boat bumped a channel marker and veered back into the middle of the waterway on its own. He didn't seem to notice.

"No sir, actually I —"

"A book then? Must be you're here because you're writing a book!"

"Well, I am kinda writing a book, but —"

"I knew it! I knew I didn't get all dressed up for somebody just wanting to bother me about some kinda nonsense."

He had the grin going again and gave the waistband of his shorts a quick adjustment before plopping into the captain's chair and grabbing the wheel just in time to miss the next channel marker.

"I bet you're wanting to hear some hair-raising stories about sharks! Am I right, or am I right?" He reached back with a bony finger and jabbed me a couple good ones in the ribs.

"Well, actually —"

"Okay, how about this? A couple years ago I was out with some clients just down from Orlando. Been to Rat World there and decided they wanted to see the real Florida. Lucky devils found out about me and booked my Lost Lunch Shark Adventure Special."

There was an old GPS unit on the instrument panel he kept looking at and tapping every once in a while.

"So we're out there at my secret shark hole, got us a big chum slick going like it's a mile-long welcome mat. It's hot, and we ain't catching shit except some small blacktips. This one boy's a big fella and he's got a smart mouth, so I told him not to hold those sharks by the tail, knowing he would. He's all full of himself since he's been to college playing football and wants to show off for his girlfriend and two buddies. So we catch another one and he grabs it by the tail to hold up for a picture. The shark ain't but about three feet long, and it flips up and takes a tiny bite clean out of this big bruiser's forearm. He goes to squealing like he was going to die. Got blood all over the little girlfriend and two buddies before we could get him patched up."

The old man eased back on the throttle and gave the GPS a good whack.

"Next, one of the buddies brings in another little shark. Big boy knows all there is about sharks now, so he grabs this one by the head and gets tail-slapped in the face and neck."

The man cut the engine to idle, then came past me out on the deck and grabbed a long pole with a hook on the end. He looked down in the water and then at me.

"Sharks got skin like sandpaper and those tail-slaps can hurt like a worst-ever case of sunburn. That big fella went to whining and crying all over again, so bad I was afraid he would scare the sharks."

Mr. Hunter's attention followed the end of the pole with the hook on it and up came a lobster trap with no buoy. I helped him drag it on deck and he pulled out lobsters and re-baited while going on with his story.

"Big'un took a break from whining about his boo-boos long enough to start in about not seeing any big sharks. That was when the wind and waves went to kicking up and a big thunderstorm started forming right on top of us. I told them folks it was time to head for the hills, but Mr. Macho wanted to stay. Sure enough, we seen a big fin coming up the chum line through the waves. Big man grabs a whole bucket of chum and dumps it over with the boat rocking and the lightning cracking around us. I didn't have a good boat like this back then, just an old scow with twin ocean-runner outboards."

After a careful look at the bottom and the GPS, the unmarked lobster trap went back over the side and three nice lobsters went in the fishbox.

"Must have been all that chum and one of the seasick buddies hanging over the side barfing got that shark excited. About the time I yelled to get the buddy back, here come the shark with a head the size of an oil drum, taking a snap at the buddy like he'd done it before. Then while the boat lurched around in the big waves and the storm got serious, the giant shark went to smashing into the boat trying to get at the snacks he'd just seen all screaming their lungs out while they were thinking maybe standing in the rollercoaster line in Orlando wasn't so bad after all."

My host and storyteller sat back in the captain's chair. When he buckled himself up with a seatbelt, I looked for something to hold onto.

"The boat was pitching around in the storm too bad to try to harpoon the shark, so I was about to bait up my biggest fishing pole when the shark stuck his head up and tried to eat one of the outboards. I couldn't see anything good coming of that, and didn't get no argument from my clients about calling it a day and heading in. By then they'd lost interest in fishing anyway and were all huddled in the cabin busy finding religion in their lives.

"The top of the outboard must not have tasted right, so that big mean bastard went to gnawing on the bottom part next. I figured he was about to chew off a prop anyway, so I fired up both two hundred and fifty horsepower engines and did some serious dental work on that shark."

Mr. Hunter hit full throttle, which seemed to signify the end of the story. The old boat shuddered a second or two before roaring up the channel. He threw off the seatbelt and motioned for me to steer the boat. While I did my best to keep from running into anything important, the old fella pulled the hatch cover off the big inboard engine which then sounded like about a million angry bees in a blender. He gave something a couple good bangs with a wrench and closed the hatch. I was happy to give back the wheel.

"'Bout never thought I'd get this damn motor running right again. Some fool offered to help me change out the turbo charger and he must have screwed with something while I wasn't looking. You ever run into somebody calls himself Slip, don't let him near no boat motors."

"Yes, sir, I'll definitely keep that in mind." He cut the throttle some as we came back toward the old marina. "What I wanted to ask you about is somebody's been leaving dead chickens outside one of the restaurants in Old Town. Wondered if you'd have any idea who might be doing something like that."

He leaned back in the captain's chair, flipped his sunglasses, and gave me a good two-count squinty look. This time with both eyes locked on me. "What makes you think I'd know anything about such nonsense as that? Somebody send you here?"

"I'm trying to find out for the lady who owns the restaurant. I been doing some asking around and your name came up. Oh, and one of the people who told me about you said to give you this." I took the little black and red voodoo doll out and tried to hand it to Shark Hunter, who jumped straight back, turned, and dove through the open window into the water.

Which, after the shock of seeing someone do such a quick and graceful exit, left me holding the doll and steering the boat again. I threw the engine out of gear and ran to the side, looking. He was treading water about fifty feet behind the boat, swimming the other way toward open water.

"Hold on, Mr. Hunter! I got you!" I spun the wheel and eased up after him. I wasn't used to the way the boat handled, so I went slow so as not to run the man over. He seemed upset enough as it was.

"I'll throw you a line!" I cut the engine so the boat would come up just a few feet from him on the starboard side. He looked back and started swimming away from the boat again. "Mr. Hunter! I'm trying to help you here! You got to swim this way, over toward the boat!"

He stopped swimming. The sunglasses came up and those eyes were hard as granite.

"You want to help me? Fine. If you got a gun on you, you can go ahead and shoot yourself in the head a few times, save me the trouble when I get back on board!"

I'd been about to throw a life jacket on a line to the man, but set it back on the deck while I thought this through. A couple of minutes later, he looked like he might be getting a bit tired of treading water. He cupped his hands around his mouth so he could give me a good yell.

"I'll tell you what, throw that damn doll off the back, as far as you can throw it, and I promise not to shoot you at all in the head."

This sounded like his final offer, so I tossed the doll, then eased the boat closer.

I got the man back aboard and he seemed to have calmed down some. He still had his cap and sunglasses but was again naked from the glasses down. He didn't say a word, went straight into the pilothouse and reached behind the seat. I thought about the gun and eased toward the side of the boat in case I deemed it prudent to take a quick dip myself. I breathed a sigh of relief when I realized he was putting his shorts back on. The sight of the little doll had literally scared him out of his britches.

He flipped up his sunglasses. "My ex-wife say anything else about me when she gave you that damn voodoo doll?"

"The woman at that store is your ex?" I'm guessing my face registered surprise.

He gave me a quick eye roll. "Of course, she's my ex. You don't think a grown man would react to a voodoo doll from anyone else that way, do you?" Before I could sort that out, he continued. "What did she say about me and chickens? She didn't say anything about me having sex with 'em or anything did she? Woman always was crazy jealous about the damnest things."

"Uh, no. She said she didn't know who'd been killing the chickens, but said you might know someone who'd do something like that."

He gave this some thought. "Well, I don't know for nothing about nobody killing no chickens. Or having sex with them for that matter." He gave me a look that was obviously meant to be sincere. "She didn't say anything about having sex with sharks, did she?"

"Uh, no."

"Good. Only people I ever heard of doing that is some crazy cult out there in California. Sex with sharks! Who ever heard of such nonsense?" The old fella got the boat going toward the dock again and looked out of the corner of his eye like he was seeing how believable that one sounded.

"So I guess you don't know anything about strange goings-on with the Blue Parrot restaurant."

He gave me a little boy shrug and smile intended to convey total innocence and ignorance. By then we were back to the narrow plank dock, so I helped tie the boat off before I left.

"Thanks for your time. I reckon I'll be going then."

"You write that book, be sure to put plenty of sex in it. And surprises. Keep 'em guessing, that's the ticket."

I thanked him again for the help and literary guidance and started up the plank.

"Hey, did you say the Blue Parrot? Man used to crew

for me years ago, I think he was working there some,
singing and playing guitar." The dog had reappeared and
was retching violently on the deck. "Got himself dead a
few days ago. That JB had the sweetest voice. Used to sing
to the sharks when we went out."

I left the old shark fisherman with his dog and his
memories. I was anxious to try out a long, hot shower.

Chapter Seven

Prior to investigating chicken murders, my life's work experience had been limited mostly to possum ranching. Though riding the possum pastures of Texas can be one of your more satisfying professions, I can't say I much minded stumbling into the fortuitous circumstances that led me to being financially independent in Key West. Between fishing, smoking fish, and doing favors for people, I managed to keep busy and mostly stay out of trouble.

"Trish, I think we may be in trouble."

It was hard to stay focused on the trouble thing while sitting across from a beautiful woman in a picturesque restaurant on a perfect day in Key West while finishing off a plate of Jerk Chicken with one hand. My client, Ms. Trish Everything, had deftly slipped a gentle hand on top of my other just as I finished filling her in on my extensive investigation and total lack of leads. The doll in her other hand faced me and seemed to speak.

"I'm sure you'll think of something. Maybe try another approach?" She pointed the doll toward a passing waitress. "June?" You really had to look hard to see her lips move. The doll faced me again. "Pie?"

"Uh, no thanks. I'm so full I could —"

"June, dear. Would you bring our guest a large slice from one of those Key Lime pies that just came out of the oven?"

I wasn't too sure about the pie. The minute I walked in the restaurant, I'd been seated at the best outside table and Trish herself had brought two steaming platters of food, which I polished off while going over the case. Investigative work can put a real appetite on you. Obviously she thought talking about it could too, and I sure didn't want to risk offending anyone by turning down food.

"So, what are you going to do?"

"I reckon I'll try a slice."

That got me an eye roll from those bright blue eyes. I noticed the doll had blue eyes too. Luckily, they didn't roll.

"About the bloody chickens!"

"Oh. Uh …," I leaned in closer, "actually, I am think- ing of another approach — a stakeout. Hide somewhere tonight and see if I can catch the person who's putting dead chickens on your doorstep."

My host and her doll leaned in close as well. "You're bloody well going to shoot the bugger, right?" She held the doll up close to my head with her index finger and thumb shooting me between the eyes. "I bloody well hope you got a big gun! Blow that bugger to bits!"

I hadn't really given much thought to what I'd do if I caught someone in the act. The only other time I'd done a similar favor on my own was looking for the missing husband of a woman who worked at the marina. Turned out he'd just run off a few miles to Marathon. Had himself a job there at a bookstore and, as I found out in a rather disturbing way, was shacked up with a goat. That bit of news wasn't too well received by the wife. She picked up a hatchet and stomped off in the general direction of Marathon. She never came back to the marina and I never saw anything in the paper, so I assumed it all worked out.

I was still getting a lethal stare from Trish and still getting shot by the doll, so I put my free hand up to ward off any further finger bullets.

"I don't know how you do things back in England, but possession of a dead chicken isn't exactly a shooting offense in the U.S. Not even in Key West."

"England? What the bloody hell makes you think I'm from England?"

"Oh, I don't know. The way you talk? The punk hairdo? The British flag on that wall over there?"

"Oh, shit. It's a long story, that." She leaned back in her chair, but her free hand stayed delicately on top of mine while I ate pie and she told me about herself.

"I was four, living with me mum over on Caroline Street when I got sick really bad. The doctor didn't think I'd make it. My mum gave me Dolly here, all porcelain from the 1800s, she is. Said she came from a British ship what wrecked out on the reef back a hundred and fifty years ago." A finger lifted the doll's dress. "As you can see, Dolly lost her knickers in the wreck." I got a rather odd wink. "I didn't die, but I didn't talk for two years, and when I did, Dolly did it for me." Like this explained everything. In the meantime, I'd about finished that generous piece of pie.

"Thanks for the great food. I reckon I'll try to catch a nap so I can come back here tonight. See what happens."

The soft hand gave a gentle squeeze, and I got a blue-eyed look of genuine concern. "Please be careful. I'd feel just bloody awful if something happened to you." She escorted me to the door with her arm through mine.

As I unlocked Rusty out on the sidewalk, something bothered me. A few minutes earlier, a scooter had come beeping by as we got to the door. I'd glanced over at the scooter as she again told me to take care and now I kept thinking it was Trish saying it, and not the doll.

I headed home for a power nap. I had to stay focused. No telling what would happen in the middle of the night.

About all that happened was it rained. And not just a light New England mist, or a Midwest dust-settler, or even a West Coast winter shower, but a true tropics frog-strangler with generous amounts of thunder and lightning. And it didn't stop either. Oh, it would slow down enough for me to be able to actually see the front of the restaurant from across the street for a few minutes, but then it would come down again harder than ever. It wasn't a night fit for man or beast, that's for sure.

My original plan had been to hide in the outdoor dining area in a place where I could see the front door, but weather conditions had me hunkered down in the home-made camper on the back of my truck. At least I'd gotten a good parking spot directly across from the restaurant. Funny how much easier parking is after midnight.

I broke camp at dawn and took it on home, but I was back more determined than ever the next night. I missed Mary Ann and wanted to get this mystery wrapped up quickly. I didn't want anything to mess up my plans to meet her for our romantic weekend coming up.

This time I had clear skies, so I hid under one of the tables outside. I thought I'd get lonely, but I had a piece of moon and a few persistent mosquitoes to keep me company. Other than the occasional traffic noise, breeze in the palms, or sudden crash, scream, or gunshot in the distance, it was a quiet night.

To pass the time I'd gone through what your typical crazed voodoo witchdoctor might likely do to anybody he found hiding under a table with only a flashlight and a bag of sunflower seeds. I'd decided he'd probably go with something like knives in the eyes or something involving fire and large pins. Not the most healthy of thoughts, but it kept me awake and alert at two a.m.

By three I was nodding. I started slipping into a dream about Mary Ann and barracuda when suddenly I was awake. A noise, behind me. My first thought was the big gun Trish had mentioned and I surely wished I had. I held perfectly still, my ears reaching out into the night. I slowly felt for my flashlight but couldn't find it. I was about to spin around and beat the tar out of whoever was behind me with a half-bag of sunflower seeds, when something cold and wet touched the back of my arm. I froze.

Turning my head slowly, I could see two yellow eyes up close. But before I could jump up and start running, something soft and wet dropped in my lap. I pushed the dead chicken off my lap and patted the dog on the head.

"Good boy."

Chapter Eight

The days that followed were filled with the kind of laughing, tanned, drink-making, fish-catching, untroubled girls who find their way to Key West every year and seem to be everywhere. That is, if you're Jimmy Redd, the marina's resident tropical vagabond who always seemed to have things going his way.

As for me, I decided it might be a good time to hunker down and take stock of things. Maybe tackle some of the repair jobs that needed doing on the old houseboat.

I also did a lot of grumbling about not getting to see Mary Ann. Her car's water pump picked a lousy time to go out. I offered to drive up to Orlando but she said someone from work with mechanic's tools was going to come over to fix it on Sunday.

I found a small patch of dry rot on the forward deck that ended up taking two days, almost a full sheet of marine plywood, and all of my patience to fix. But at least it took my mind off things for a while. I had just retired to the upper deck with a cold beer to enjoy the late afternoon breeze and watch the final coat of epoxy dry, when Slip showed up.

"Hey, Taco. Consuelo said to give you this."

I took the offered paper bag and inside was a book, *Tastes Like Chicken — 101 Fowl Recipes.*

Slip helped himself to a chair and came up with his own beer and a wide grin. The jokes had about played out in my opinion.

"Very funny. Tell Consuelo —"

"Tell Consuelo what?" Behind Slip a blond head popped up, followed by the rest of a very familiar female form coming up the ladder. "Oh, what's that book you have in your hand, Capt Bob? Someone must have a naughty sense of humor to give you that! Whoever it is probably needs to be disciplined!"

Consuelo turned and offered a shapely rear within easy reach. Slip and I glanced at the hot pink shorts stretched tight across tanned and toned girl flesh, then concentrated on our beers.

"You catch that ball game on TV last night?"

"Nah, after working on the boat all day, I decided to turn in early. I heard on the radio this morning, though, that our boys won."

"Yep, pulled it out in the end like the true champions they are."

Our sexy friend gave up and turned around with her arms folded across her chest. Actually, they were folded under her halter top so everything pushed up and you could see the tan line across her breasts. I tried not to look.

"You guys are so full of shit. The only sports on late last night involving balls were golf reruns and bowling.

And speaking of a lack of balls," she fixed a hard stare on Slip, "what did you find out about this creep?" A finger pointed over her shoulder in the direction of the fancy houseboat three doors down.

Slip pulled out a pocket notebook and flipped some pages while giving Consuelo a couple of warning squints.

"Since we're all wondering who the dime-dropping shitheel is who's been sending the po-lice over here with false reports, I've taken it upon myself" — Consuelo had been leaning against the rail, but pushed herself standing and started a low growl — "at the insistence of this fine young lady"— Consuelo eased back — "to make some discreet inquiries around the marina."

Consuelo took it.

"Yeah, I told Columbo here to ask around. Thought maybe the old dude in the marina office knows something about the jerkball on the Busted Flusher or whatever he calls it."

Slip made a show of clearing his throat as he consulted his notebook.

"The lowlife in question is Harry Grizzel. He's thirty-nine, a lawyer." Slip spit over the railing. "Did a two-year jolt in Stark back in the late '80s for fencing stolen property and domestic violence. After that he decided crime didn't pay, enough, and got a job as a telemarketer selling phony extended warranties on electronic equipment to pay his way through lawyer school.

"Graduated from the East Haiti School of Law and Auto Repair at the bottom of his class, headed for New Jersey, and got into the lucrative world of insurance fraud. While hanging with the bottom feeders up there, he got some work with the wise guys in New York." A bigger spit over the side this time. "He showed up in Key West a year ago when things got too hot up north. Now he specializes in cash-only work for the shoe-scrapings of society, like Internet spammers, check washers, child molesters, and insurance companies. Recently he's also dipped a toe into the scum pond of real estate development."

I thought there might be more spitting, but we just got the tight-lipped cold stare Slip only breaks out for special occasions — like any mention of the kind of lower life-forms who prey on the old and infirm. I was impressed by all that he'd learned.

"That's a mighty in-depth report, Slip. I'm surprised the old guy at the marina would even come upon knowing such things, much less pass them along. Always seemed a mean ol' cuss to me."

Consuelo motioned to Slip for a sip of his beer. She must have been impressed by Slip's findings as well since she didn't have any of her usual wise cracks. Slip hesitated, but handed his beer over and hitched his pants a little.

"Well, the old fart pretty much just said Grizzel's boat slip was paid up a year in advance by some company, and since he knows I do some guiding, he took the opportunity to ask where he might find some redfish next week when his brother came to town. I asked him what company paid Grizzel's bill and he said none of my business, so I told him to try the Key West Aquarium on Whitehead for reds."

Consuelo handed back the empty and crushed beer-can. She locked on Slip.

"So where did you dig up the dirt on the creep? From the big furry guy, I bet. The one with the thick pelt of gray hair they call Meyers." Consuelo gave me a conspiratorial wink. "Everybody tells Meyers their deepest, darkest."

It was true. There always seemed to be someone on his stout little boat *Maynard G Krebs* having a heart-felt talk. Nobody knew the big bear of a man's real name or where he came from, they just called him Meyers after the brand of rum he favored.

"Yeah, Meyers said our man Grizzel showed up at his place drunk one night with a bottle of tequila. Wanted the old fella to fix him up with a woman, since there always seems to be young ladies hanging around there. Grizzel ended up telling his life story, then ralphing all over the *Maynard* before passing out." Slip started in inspecting his fingernails like he hadn't seen them in a long time. I took the bait.

"So I'm assuming he told you something else? Something to make you think neighbor Harry Grizzel is the one responsible for those calls?"

Slip looked up like he'd forgotten we were there. "Something else? Oh yeah, he had plenty more to say. Things like Grizzel can't handle his liquor, has been doing some kind of illegal wire taps for big money, and is blind jealous over seeing Miss Manners here jiggling down the dock everyday on her way over to your boat."

Consuelo quickly withdrew the little finger that had covertly begun to explore her left nostril.

"Yeah, I've seen him watching me. Tried to talk me into checking out his houseboat once. Offered me a drink with some kind of gin I never heard of and said he had some great stories about the 'salvage game.' Real creep." She stuck out her tongue and made a face.

Slip had more. "Meyers said the man is trying to live like a fictional character out of some book. He said the name but I didn't write it down." He held up his notebook and shook it like a TV evangelist. "I think the guy's got a screw loose when it comes to women and goes ballistic at any sign of rejection." Slip slapped his notebook closed and looked at Consuelo.

"Hey, he comes on about as sincere as a used-car salesman on crank. No woman in her right mind would have anything to do with a creep like that." Consuelo turned from Slip to me, "Anyway, I've got like a sixth sense when it comes to men. I usually know a loser before he even opens his mouth. I also know when I'm around a real man." I got an intense, doe-eyed look that could mean only one thing to any male with a pulse. I tried to get things back on track.

"Well, it sounds like he's likely the one's been doing it then. I reckon I should have a talk with the man."

My companions looked at me like I'd lost my mind. Both started to say something, but I held up a hand. "I'm sure you two can cook up the kind of dirty tricks Fox could make a TV series about, but you need to let me talk to the man first. Okay?" Unconvinced looks all around. "No exploding buckets of rotten fish, letters from AIDS clinics, or sinking boats. Agreed?"

Slip couldn't stand it. "How about just give him one quick ass-whupping?" Balled up fists.

"No."

"How about if Blondie does it?"

Consuelo tried an innocent look.

"No. You both just behave. I'm sure I can talk some sense into the man. Anyway, we're not one hundred per-cent sure he's the one making those calls." Both started to protest but held when I raised my hand again. "You two give me a minute to take a shower and I'll treat at Floaters." The mention of our favorite cheap restaurant seemed to console them for the moment.

As I headed below to clean up, I could hear Consuelo say to Slip in a low, menacing voice that she does not "jiggle."

Chapter Nine

Floaters Restaurant had sunk again so we went to Governor's. There was a Governor's Chicken Burritos just opened on Duval with the new menu we'd heard about. Besides the old favorites, there were some new items to choose from:

Chicken or the Egg
chicken omelet
Offroad
garden salad with roasted chicken strips
Eighteen-Wheeler
platter of wings in red sauce
Skidmark
bacon strips on a chicken patty
Road Gravel
peas and rice with chicken
Hit and Run
chicken-feet soup
Speed Bumps
chicken link sausages
Chicken That Almost Crossed the Road
jalapeno and chicken poppers
Blowout
deluxe platter, a generous sample of everything

We got our orders figured out finally, and the food came served up on a plate that looked like a hubcap. On closer inspection, it was a hubcap. We dug in.

"The funeral's tomorrow morning, you know."

I had forgotten until Slip mentioned it. "Slipped my mind. You two going?"

A couple of grunts in the affirmative from my table mates, both very involved in developing a close personal relationship with their food. We had a booth by the front window, and Consuelo boob-speared me in the shoulder reaching for the pepper. I set the rest of the condiments in front of her and she blushed a little.

"I told my sisters I need the car tomorrow. The funeral is scheduled for ten. You guys want me to pick you up at the marina?"

Sounded fine to me. "Sure. You good with that, Slip?" A nod and a grunt. "No sense in us getting there too early, it's not like we're family or anything."

Consuelo had gone back to eating but came up for air. "Yeah, all we did was find the guy all bloated and stinking with his skin splitting open and his eyeballs falling out and stuff. It's not like we were close." She waved something that resembled a chicken leg in my face for emphasis. "You know, it's been almost a week, I hope they did something so he doesn't smell so bad."

There was a muffled noise behind me and the two young women from the next booth left abruptly. Consuelo reached over to their table for two pieces of untouched chicken and gave me another spearing in the arm. She handed one piece over to Slip, who didn't even look up, just grabbed it and started gnawing.

Consuelo glanced back over her shoulder, "Wonder what their problem is?"

Slip took a swallow of beer, "Probably too much sun, makes 'em flighty like that." He motioned to the waitress across the room. "Bet they're kindergarten teachers. Saw in the paper there's a whole convention of them in town this week. Since I'll be all dressed up for the funeral tomorrow, maybe afterwards I'll go by the hotel where they're all staying and see what happens."

The waitress started over for our dessert order.

"Yep, ain't nothing in the whole world like a sunburned kindergarten teacher. I heard rubbing a stick of butter on sunburn is a mild aphrodisiac. I get all frisky just thinking about it." Slip smiled big at the waitress looking down at us with a sour expression, "Imagine we'll each have a piece of your famous gizzard pie." He checked our nodding heads and the waitress left.

Consuelo was looking out the window.

"Hey, isn't that Jimmy Redd in that convertible with the blond? The one parked across the street?"

We took a peek. I couldn't really tell.

"Might be. Man always seems to travel in fine company."

Consuelo gave me a look, "And you don't?"

She laid her head on my shoulder, snuggled a bit, and belched. I patted her on the head, then pushed her back up straight, "But you're the fairest of them all."

"Ah, you say the sweetest things, Taco." She gave me the fluttering eyelashes.

Slip was still looking out the window.

"Yeah, that's him. Good-looking woman, all right. Not my type though. I like my women with some meat on their bones. Damn, but I can't seem to stop thinking about slippery pink kindergarten teachers."

Slip's upper half was still eating, but his legs were twitching so much the table started to shake. Consuelo picked up her almost full water glass and pointed it at Slip. The twitching stopped. I noticed Jimmy and his lady friend had gotten out and walked over to where a Marty Manatee stood singing and playing guitar on the corner. I'd lay odds by the size of the crowd that had gathered up all of a sudden that the song was "Tequila Breakfast."

Our dessert arrived and Slip wrapped his in a napkin and stood up. "I think I'll ease on over and see if I can catch a ride with Jimmy. Maybe get him to drop me off at that convention hotel." And headed for the door.

Consuelo gave him a yell, "Hey! Nine-thirty tomorrow morning!"

"No problem! Thanks for the dinner, Taco!"

I slid my pie across the table then took Slip's seat. Consuelo started to protest, but gave it a rest for once. She did try a small pout though.

"It's not like I bite."

I dove into my pie and watched Slip talking to Jimmy across the street. Consuelo gave up the act and started in on her own dessert.

"Hey, TB, what's the deal with Jimmy anyway? I heard he used to live up north? Hard to believe, looks like a conch if I ever saw one."

"You know how you hear about some people are lucky? Jimmy's one of those people, though he says he wasn't like that before coming to the Keys."

It was one of your more popular stories around the marina, so I was surprised Consuelo didn't know it.

"Way I heard it, he lived someplace way up north like Toronto, Canada. Every day he drove to the same crappy job on the same road, and every day he fantasized about turning south and just driving until he ran out of road. Then one day he hauled off and did it.

"Drove all night and all day and fell asleep in his car right over there at the marina. He woke up when the big boat he'd parked next to fired up its engines at four in the morning. He wandered over and talked to the captain waiting for his crew. They never showed, so Jimbo hired on for a week of grouper fishing."

I looked up from my pie at Consuelo, who had a large lemon slice clamped in her teeth and was giving me a bright yellow grin. I took this as a compliment on my narrative and continued.

"Turns out the grouper they were after were the highly prized, though highly illegal, Square Grouper, a species that usually migrates from places like Columbia on big rusty tankers. The way Jimmy told it, the freighter was a few days late, so while they sat out there offshore, the captain taught him how to play guitar. They finally loaded the boat so full it was about to sink, and stoned to the gills they came easing back in. Almost made it, too."

Consuelo had both hands in her lap, doing something.

"Got just off Sombrero Key and lost the boat in a bad squall. Jimmy and the captain washed ashore along with most of the pot, and Jimmy's share was enough to buy a boat of his own. Several trips offshore later, he had enough money saved to retire in style, so instead he proceeded to set the World Land Speed Record for Pissing Away Money. In a few weeks he was as broke as the day he fell asleep in his car at the marina."

The waitress came by and started taking the plates. Consuelo showed the lady her hand.

"Could I get a clean fork? This one's dirty."

A fork seemed to be sticking out of her hand, complete with very realistic-looking ketchup blood dripping on the table. The waitress gave me a tired look, then retrieved the fork and carried it off with the dirty dishes. Consuelo stuck her tongue out at the departing waitress then stared at me with exaggerated attention.

"So how did Jimmy Redd get that cute little sailboat, the *Herring*?"

"The upside of going through that much money that quick is, Jimmy made a lot of friends in every bar in town. He started playing guitar in bars, and with his luck holding, a vacationing big-time record-industry type seen him one night at the Hog's Breath Saloon and signed him on the spot. Jimmy flew out to California, cut a record, and came back to Key West with a nice check. The next day the big shot was arrested in some kind of payola bust, made bail, and cut town. No one knows what happened to the guy or the record. In the meantime Jimmy bought a sailboat with the money." I finished off my dessert just in time to wrap up the story.

"These days the man's happy as a beaver with a chainsaw. Always sitting around in the shade with a lazy smile and a drink in his hand, or strumming that guitar for some young ladies over on his boat."

Consuelo was giving her drink straw a slow lick, "Yeah, us young ladies like a man with a big, uh, boat."

I rolled eyes at my tablemate, then spied the waitress across the room.

"Check, please!"

I had to make a run up to the marine supply store in Marathon and, on the way back, got to once again experience a phenomenon unique to the Keys. Since U.S. Highway 1 is the only road and a lot of it is still two lanes, any kind of serious wreck, especially on a bridge, is an automatic and often prolonged timeout for traffic in both directions. I usually keep a crossword puzzle book as well as a spinning rod and reel in my truck for just that reason.

So whenever traffic stops, everybody pretty much just shuts their vehicle off right away. Some get out and walk up and down the row of cars to visit with people they know. Small groups usually form around anyone with a CB radio, trying to find out what's going on causing the jam.

I kicked back and did a few crosswords, since where I'd stopped wasn't much of a place to fish.

A few weeks earlier I'd been in a similar situation a bit further down the road near Bahia Honda. That day it was almost dark and it looked like a long one. Since there was a dire shortage of restrooms in the vicinity, I grabbed my fishing pole and went to kill a couple of birds.

With my fishing pole under one arm I was hiding behind some mangroves adding to the tide when I heard a moan mixed in with the waves lapping the shore. I ignored the sound, figured a sea bird or such, but when I heard it again I turned on my little flashlight. I could barely see a hand sticking out of the mangrove branches. I would have called 911 right then, but I'd left my cell in the truck.

I got my feet wet fighting my way into the mangroves, and the guy was a real mess. Older man, wispy gray hair and skin to match. The only color on his face a big blue crab with its claws out defending its prize. He was so tangled in branches I wasn't about to try to get him out, but got the crab off and tried to get him to come to. All I got was more moaning.

"You hang in there, partner. I'll go see about getting some help." I started to straighten up and go for the phone when a hand grabbed my ankle.

"Wait!"

Sounded like he gave it his all and it still came out raspy and weak. I told the old guy everything would be okay, I'd just go call the cops and be right back.

"No cops!"

For someone who looked so dead, he had a very persuasive grip on my ankle. He let go, grabbed my shirt next, and pulled me down close to his face.

"Get me out of here. Just you, no cops!"

My first thought was the bottle of Scope with the groceries back in my truck. My second thought was from now on I'd try fishing on the other side of the road.

He rallied a bit and talked me into dragging him out of the thicket. He came out easier after I used my folding pliers and knife tool to cut the wire holding the concrete block to his feet. His wrists had also been wired together.

After I got him laid out on a comfortable piece of sand-spur–covered ground, I went to get the phone and drove my truck off to the side of the road since traffic had started to move. I brought him some water and a little food. He told me a number to call and took the phone when someone answered. I had to tell him where we were, then he told someone to come pick him up. After the old fella gave my phone back, he asked if it would have that number in its memory. I checked and told him yes. He said to memorize the number and then erase it from the phone. So I did, while he ate some crackers and drank some water. He had to be in a lot of pain but seemed to revive some.

When asked, I told him I lived in Key West and aspired to be a writer. A wiry hand pulled me close.

"Sooner or later you'll be blocked. It'll come up when you least expect it and bite you on the ass. You have to fight back then, and do what desperate men have always done — steal!"

He grabbed my arm and looked at my watch. "You need to get out of here."

He didn't have to say it twice. I stood to leave but he had one more thing to say.

"You ever need anything, anything at all, you just call that number. I owe you big."

We exchanged names and handshakes.

And that was how I met Anthony Cravinino, whom the media dubbed Tony the Crab during the mob war that started the next week.

Chapter Ten

It wasn't bad as far as funerals go. JB had a lot of friends and would be missed. Despite the bluebird skies and gentle breeze, the funeral had put a pall on the day. Funerals are like that.

Consuelo dropped me at the marina then took off with Slip. To drop him at the convention hotel would be my guess.

I opened up the old houseboat, and since funerals tend to make me thirsty, I headed for the beer locker. Home never looked so good since Consuelo had come down with a case of the domestics the day before and tidied the place up while I was gone to the marine supply store.

Beer in hand, I plopped on the comfy old couch and had a long, slow swallow. I looked up at the shelf where I kept the statues and they were gone. The service for JB had brought back the memory of our rather unsettling discovery out on the water, and I'd only been about half listening to Consuelo coming back in the car. When I saw a row of books on the shelf instead of the three little idols,

I remembered she'd said something about putting them in a safer place. I just didn't remember where. I changed clothes and spent the rest of the day sanding and painting an area on the upper deck.

That night I was lying in bed thinking about the rather short phone conversation I'd had earlier with Mary Ann. I was about to drop off when I felt the slightest movement on the boat. I had company.

I eased out of the big bed, slipped on some shorts, then found my heavy cop flashlight right where it was supposed to be. The club shape of the light felt reassuring in a primeval way. Peeking out a window I could just make out a dark figure on the back deck. A woman, looking undecided about knocking on the cabin door. I kept the lights off and went into the main room. My big toe sent me a sudden and very painful reminder that Consuelo had moved some furniture during her cleaning frenzy. Even though I was expecting a knock on the door, the sharp rapping came just as I was suppressing a banged-toe yelp and startled me enough that I made a sound not unlike the yip a small dog would make.

"Anyone home? Taco Bob, are you in there?"

I limped over and cracked the door an inch.

"Taco Bob? My name is Julie Brown. I know it's late, but can I come in? I really need to talk to you."

I flipped on a light and gestured toward the couch with the flashlight, which I then noticed had somehow turned into the big sex toy Slip found in the clothes locker once. I wasn't the only one to notice.

"I hope I'm not interrupting."

Now she was looking at my shorts, which I realized were on backwards. I reached behind and zipped them up.

"I need to ask you something important, but if you need a minute."

I mumbled about being right back and limped into the bedroom.

While making some wardrobe adjustments and getting my bed hair under control, I made a mental note not to let Consuelo clean up anymore. I still had to find out what she'd done with my flashlight.

After I made myself a bit more presentable and did a quick toe inspection — bruised, but not broken — I went back to my late-night guest. A mighty fine-looking guest I might add, still sitting on the couch and looking around the room.

"Do you have a dog? I thought I heard a dog."

"Uh, no. That was my, uh, doorbell. What did you say your name was?"

The young lady not only looked fine, with dark hair down past her shoulders and big brown eyes, but she also looked familiar.

"Julie Brown, I'm JB's sister."

Bingo. Except now she didn't have the big hat and sunglasses, though she was still dressed in black.

"You were at the funeral today."

"Yes. I'm real sorry about your loss. I didn't know JB, but folks around here spoke well of him."

She seemed nervous, so I went into the galley. Nothing calms like refreshments.

"I heard you're the one who found his body."

I set up a tray with sodas, crackers, and fish spread. I had to talk loud from the galley.

"Offshore. But it's not something I want to go into, and I'm pretty sure it's not something you want to hear about." I came back into the lounge and set the tray on the coffee table in front of the couch, then took a chair within easy reach.

"That's not why I came here, Mr. Bob."

I motioned toward the refreshments, and she didn't hesitate to dive in.

"Please, call me Taco."

"Okay, Taco." She started smiling and making little moans of approval at the spread. She loaded up another cracker and so did I.

"This is really good! Did you make this?"

"As a matter of fact," I unfurled my best modest smile. "So, Julie. It's Julie, right?"

She gave me a nod and a dismissive wave. We were both going at the crackers and spread. I was glad I'd decided to bring out a full pint container. At one point we both went after the spread knife, I gave her a sweeping, ladies first bow and saw a quick smile, there and gone.

"So, Julie, you heard about my famous smoked-fish spread and decided to stop by in the middle of the night, is that it?"

We both had a good nervous laugh and she started loading up another cracker.

"Oh, no. I just wanted to tell you, I think I know who killed my brother. They tried to kill me and will probably come after you next."

Ten minutes later, after we'd determined that I most likely wasn't going to die from gagging on a spread-laden cracker, I asked her if she could perhaps elaborate.

"JB had a lot of friends, but he had some enemies too. You probably know he was planning to run for mayor next year."

I gave a nod from the floor like who didn't know that.

"Some of his campaign promises were upsetting people. One thing he wanted was more health department inspections of the bars. He also vowed to rid Key West of voodoo and ban shark fishing."

I looked up from cleaning the floor of the refreshments I'd sprayed a few minutes earlier. "I can see where that might tend to get certain folks a mite upset." Or a lot upset.

"And he wanted to clamp down on the realtors and developers. Especially the ones planning the big project off the southern end of the island."

This I had heard about. According to the newspaper, a big developer had found a way to overcome Key West's biggest real estate problem — the lack of available land to build on. At one time Hong Kong had a similar problem, so they brought in a huge amount of fill dirt and built a few square miles of land for their new airport. Supposedly, the developer for the Key West project planned to do the same thing, just on a much smaller scale. Rumors had the developer buying an island in the Bahamas and barging it over to take advantage of a loophole in the dredging laws. I couldn't see how they'd ever get past the environmentalists with something like that though.

However, I sure could see where it would be a developer's wet dream — acres of bare land in one of the most choice, not to mention expensive, places in the country.

"So you think someone killed your brother because of his upcoming political campaign?" Before she could answer, I had more. "Maybe first you should tell me about someone trying to kill you, and why you think your brother's death wasn't an accident. The last I heard, the official cause of death was drowning, and the police didn't have any reason to suspect foul play."

"Well, my brother was an excellent swimmer." Like that explained everything. She'd gone back to eating spread and crackers. "And a few days ago, when I was driving here from Miami to take care of my brother's things, a big truck almost ran me off the road as I was going up on one of the bridges. I hope you don't mind, this stuff really is great."

"No, you can have my share, I seem to have lost my appetite." She was really wolfing the stuff down. "So you think your brother was murdered because he drowned and the big truck was the same people?"

"Of course! What other explanation could there be?" I could think of several right off. "And before you ask, I did tell the police about it and they said they'd get back with me. They never did."

"And you think someone might be out to get me as well?"

She had a loaded cracker in each hand and some spread on her chin. "Well, you did find the body. I saw a movie once where the killer went after the person who found the body. It makes perfect sense."

I looked at the clock on the wall. It was getting late. "Julie, you've been under a lot of pressure lately, and a good night's sleep might not be a bad idea. Get yourself some rest and things will probably look a lot better tomorrow." I noticed she'd eaten almost the whole bowl of spread. "Where are you staying?"

"At my brother's house, over by the Southernmost Hotel." She gave me the sad eyes. "You think I'm crazy, don't you?"

"No, I think you've probably been through a lot the last few days. Do you have a car?"

She nodded and looked about to cry as I got out my card.

"Look, here's my phone number. Get some sleep and give me a call in the morning if you want to. I can stop by, I've got friends I haven't seen in a while who work in that area. I was planning on bringing them some spread sometime in the next couple of days anyway."

She managed to hold back the tears and came over and gave me a big hug.

"Thanks for letting me talk. I really appreciate your listening to me so late like this."

I walked her out to her car, where I got an even bigger hug and a promise she'd get some sleep then call me in the morning.

Chapter Eleven

"I got a nice tip yesterday guiding. How about we head over to Gov's? My treat."

"As tempting as that sounds, I think I should stick around a while longer. I'm expecting a call."

"You? You're buying?"

Consuelo had been working on a sulk since I'd mentioned as delicately as I could about her not cleaning up the houseboat anymore. Even changing that to at least not moving the furniture hadn't helped, so I was glad Slip had come up with his unheralded offer. It got her thinking about something else.

"Taco, whoever it is can just leave a message. We don't dare miss out on this." She turned a fierce look on Slip. "You really have money? This isn't some kind of joke?"

Slip pulled a handful of bills from his shorts. My turn to get the fierce look from under blond hair.

"Consuelo, can we give it ten more minutes? If she doesn't call by then, we can try to find her place before we go eat."

"She?" Both of them saying it at the same time.

"I had a visitor last night."

Slip motioned for a time-out and ran down the ladder. Consuelo practiced giving me a dirty look, while I tried to ignore her and look around at the comings and goings of the marina from the upper deck of my houseboat on yet another perfect postcard day in the tropics. Slip came back and generously offered me one of my own beers, then one for our frowning companion, before opening one for himself.

"Do tell?"

"Late, after twelve, JB's sister, Julie, came by."

Consuelo softened considerably, "Oh, we saw her at the funeral yesterday. The poor thing looked pretty shaken."

"Well, she told me last night she thinks someone murdered her brother." I let that sit a beat. "Said it might have something to do with JB running for mayor next time. She also thinks the same people tried to force her car off the road when she drove down here from Miami." Still no comment. "Said the reason she came here last night was to warn me. I guess she'd seen some movie once where a killer came after the person who found the body. I told the poor girl to get some sleep and give me a call when she got up this morning if she wanted to talk. Now that I think about it, she more than likely won't call. Probably woke up embarrassed she came by so late with such a wild story."

My companions hadn't moved a muscle — glued to my every word. Consuelo finally spoke up.

"I saw that movie a few years ago. Three people found the body. The killer got them one at a time."

Slip cleared his throat and sat up straighter in his chair. "I seen that one too. I think it was *Kitchen Psycho 2*. Guy used a carrot peeler on one of 'em. Scared me so bad I peed the bed that night and couldn't look at a carrot for weeks."

"At least I didn't pee the bed," Consuelo gave Slip an off look for his unmanly confession, "though it did give my little sister nightmares for a long time. Come to think about it, that might be part of the reason she turned out so weird."

This reminded me of the doozy of a nightmare I'd had after Julie left. Time to change the subject.

"Well, before we get ourselves any more creeped out, how about we see if we can find JB's place, check on his sister, and then see how much of Slip's hard-earned we can spend at Governor's."

We dropped a bowl of spread off at the seashell stand of some friends and got directions to JB's place. It was a small house mostly hidden with tropical vegetation at the end of a street and right on the water. Julie's little red car was parked in front. We tried knocking and checked around the house. Nobody home. This I didn't like. She should have been there.

"I still can't believe you two would be so worried about something you saw in a movie."

I'd been having some cautious fun with my two associates while hitting the high points of Julie's visit at their urging. Cautious because it was unlike them to take something like this seriously.

But I was getting some mighty serious looks over a table full of Governor's finest eats. So serious Slip hadn't once mentioned kindergarten teachers, and even though Consuelo had again worked it so she was sitting next to me in the booth, she hadn't once bumped, rubbed, or leaned against me. Serious.

Slip glanced around him to make sure no one was listening in. "Taco, maybe you should tell us about those campaign promises you mentioned. Might give us a little to go on here. Maybe somebody did whack ol' JB."

I decided to play along. Maybe they'd see the foolishness of it all. "Well, it sounds like JB wanted to do something about that big project we keep hearing about for adding onto the island. That, and she said something about more inspections for the bars and banning shark fishing. JB also wanted to shut down the voodoo folks."

Consuelo wiggled around a bit in the seat next to me before she spoke. "Not that I'm any expert on politics, but that doesn't sound like the usual ass-kissing, make-nice, talk-a-lot-and-say-nothing campaigns most people running for office come up with."

Slip was about to nod his head completely off. "Yeah, exactly! He might have been about to stomp on the wrong toes, so somebody took him out!" Slip made his point while gesturing with what resembled a chicken wing. Barbeque sauce was coming off the end of it like the Pope anointing someone with holy water. I got a few drops on my plate, but some speckled the sleeve of Consuelo's new white blouse. She didn't seem to notice but held a mustard dispenser while she talked.

"What about the police? Did Julie tell them about the truck?" She put a generous dab of mustard on a fingernail and deftly flipped it. Got Slip right between the eyes. He didn't even blink, just sat there with a big yellow splatter on his forehead.

"She told me the police didn't seem to be particularly interested. The last I heard, there wasn't any reason to suspect foul play and JB's death was considered to be a drowning."

This brought some snorts, grumbles, and at least one, "Yeah, right." One of Slip's hands started easing slowly for the squeeze bottle of ketchup while he talked. "The po-lice ain't going to do squat. We got a dead Marty Manatee, probably murdered, an attempt on his sister, who I might add is currently mysteriously missing, and three folks who found the body, who if they don't do something real soon might be waking up one morning on the wrong end of a carrot peeler!"

I held a menu open over the table between them just as Slip's hand got to the ketchup and Consuelo snatched up a bowl of gravy.

"You folks needing anything else?"

We each gave the waitress a big smile. I handed Slip a napkin and Consuelo asked for some club soda for her blouse. The waitress left and my tablemates exchanged warning looks.

I was far from convinced. "I can't believe you two are getting so worked up. How's this: We finish this fine fare, stop by and talk to Julie so you can see there's nothing to worry about, then take the Wilbur out and do some fishing?"

The mention of fishing had everyone in a better mood. We cleaned our plates and headed over to Julie's.

Julie wasn't there. Her car was still out front, but my feeble theory about her being out for a walk didn't seem to carry much weight with my colleagues. As I feared, Slip had been thinking.

"Taco, we need to take the bull by the horns here. Much as I'd like to go fishing, I think we ought to do a little checking around. See if there might be a way we can avoid ending up like poor ol' JB."

Consuelo's new lacy top had cleaned up just fine. She looked quite fetching standing there in the sunshine by JB's cottage. She also looked like she agreed with Slip, nodding her head as he spoke. So much for fishing.

"Okay, I give up. What do you have in mind?"

The man who'd once eaten twenty-three hotdogs in a contest, then mounted the plastic trophy to the bow of his kayak, had been quiet driving over from the restaurant. He'd obviously been doing some hard planning. We stepped into the shade of a small tree and Slip started pacing.

"We split up, do some discreet inquiries around town, see if maybe JB got somebody riled enough they'd be wanting to make sure his upcoming campaign platform never got much airplay." He stopped pacing in front of me. "Taco, you check out your buddy Shark Hunter. Princess Leia here can see what that voodoo gal you seen before has to say for herself, and I'll start checking the bars."

Consuelo got it before I could. "No way you're getting the bars and I'm hanging around some dusty old spook shop!"

I held up a hand. "I'll go visit Mr. Hunter. Consuelo, Ms. Levita didn't seem to much like me, and you're good with older people. I bet she'd tell you things she wouldn't tell Slip or me." While that was taking root, I had something I knew she'd like. "How about if Slip checks the newspaper and county records for info on the big development. We can all meet late this afternoon at Pirate Jim's and ask Fish Daddy about those bar inspections. Seems like someone who spends all his time in bars might know a thing or two about that."

Slip wasn't too excited about the agenda but got voted down. We agreed on a time to meet and headed for the truck. The same convertible we'd seen before came around the corner just then with Jimmy Redd behind the wheel. He pulled over and stopped next to my truck. Slip looked happy to see him.

"Jimbo! Where's your girlfriend? You going by the courthouse by chance?"

Slip jumped in the front seat and started fumbling with the seat belt before Jimmy could answer. The man who lived a life right out of a song looked over at us and shrugged, gave up a smile, then headed out with Slip talking a mile a minute about murders and carrot peelers. Consuelo watched them go a little before getting in the truck.

"Taco, did Jimmy look nervous to you?"

"I don't know. But he *has* been acting a bit strange lately."

"Can you drop me at the hotel?" Consuelo and her sisters ran a small hotel in Old Town.

"You going to get your bike?"

"Nah, I need to change clothes. I feel like a run."

Chapter Twelve

Unfortunately, Mr. Hunter wasn't on his boat, which meant another trip to the Scorpion Pit.

Looked like about the same lineup of regulars inside, the same skitterish young bartender, but luckily, no Robert. I bellied up to the bar.

"Shark Hunter around?"

The bartender dropped an empty glass. It bounced once off the wooden duckboards before shattering on the concrete floor. "Upstairs," he stood pointing toward the stairs. "You going up there?" He gave me a hopeful look. Just then there was a thunderous yell from above.

"BEER!"

The hopeful look turned to more like pleading. The young fella pointed to a full pitcher. I got the idea.

"You want me to take that upstairs?"

A series of quick little nods.

"Whatever you want for yourself, mister, on the house."

I took my free draft and headed upstairs with the pitcher.

I had to stop for a second at the top of the stairs and take stock of the scene before me. The flat roof of the bar was black tar with a knee-high concrete wall all around. A couple of sunshades and several tables and chairs lay scattered amongst the debris and broken glass near where I stood. On the far side, closest to the water, a big tree shaded more of the same. The same except for one upright table, several bloody human corpses, and Shark Hunter. He was leaning back in his chair against the low wall, reading a book. He looked up, smiled, and waved.

I made my way through the debris and stood across the table from the man. A body lay at my feet, blood all over its face and chest.

"I remember you! Taco Something, right?"

He put the book down and stuck his hands out toward me, fingers wiggling. I handed over the pitcher.

"Yes, sir. Taco Bob, actually. You been having some trouble here?"

He took a long drink right from the pitcher and looked genuinely puzzled. "Trouble? No, just been partying a little with my crew and clients."

I noticed the bloody body slouched in a chair next to Mr. Hunter was snoring softly.

"Where's my manners? I should introduce you." He turned loose a sizable belch. "That there by your feet is Mr. Peters. Big-time lawyer from Boston. The one curled up under the table is his son, Ben."

The old shark man was slurring his words a little. I figured he must have been drinking for a while.

"This sizable creature here is my deck hand, Baby. Hey, Taco, no need to stand on ceremony." He reached over to hold the chair and gave Baby a push with his bare foot. The unconscious man thudded to the floor. "Have a seat."

I did, carefully.

"And this here is my best drinking buddy, Moe." He looked behind to his right, then his left, then stood suddenly, panicked. "Where's Moe? He was here a minute ago!" Standing so quick seemed to make the man dizzy, his eyes rolled back in his head a little.

"Mr. Hunter! Are you all right?" I stood to steady him, but he spun around and started heaving over the side of the building.

After a couple of minutes of violent retching, he called down to the ground, "Sorry about that Moe! Didn't see you there. I guess you fell off again? Wave if you're okay. Good man. You just lay there and rest then, I'll come hose you down later." He turned back around with a big smile. "Now, where were we?"

"Your friend okay?"

"Sure, bushes broke his fall. Told him not to sit on the wall. Luckily he's drunk as a skunk or he might have got hurt." He gestured with his hand in the general direction of the other three, "Stone drunk, the lot of 'em."

"Are they hurt? There's a lot of blood."

"Nah. We had us a big night on the water, tied into some mighty fine sharks. Kept one little two-hundred-pound nurse shark. Gave most of it to a local charity and Baby kept the liver. He told Big and Little Peters here it's manly to eat it raw; showed 'em how. Amazing what men, even ones who normally show some small amount of common sense, will do after drinking a quart of tequila, especially when their manliness is called into question." He looked at his unconscious clients, then slapped his forehead. "I forgot my manners again!" He opened a cooler and shoved it closer. "There's plenty left if you'd care to partake?" Several red hunks floating in blood.

"I just ate, but thanks anyway."

"Baby swears by it." He glanced in the cooler, shrugged his shoulders, then slammed the lid. "I never touch the stuff myself, makes me shit like a goose."

"Mr. Hunter, I was wanting to ask you something."

"You ain't got any more voodoo dolls from my ex? You do, we got to go out to my truck so I can shoot you. Prissy little bartender won't let me bring guns in anymore."

"No sir, no dolls. I wanted to ask you about JB. I heard he wanted to ban shark fishing if he got to be mayor. Thought since you knew the man and are an expert on all things shark, you might know about that."

I got the thing with the eyes again — one staring at me while the other gave me a good going-over.

"You got some of the damnedest questions! Last time it was chicken sacrifices as I remember. You don't have the smell of a cop. This all for that book you're writing?"

"No, sir. JB's sister told me she suspected he'd been murdered and the same folks might be after her. She also said the one's found the body might be in danger, which would be me."

"You found the body? Paper said he'd been in the water a few days. Was he all —"

"The body was in pretty bad shape."

The old fella gave this some hard consideration. "So I bet you're thinking if you find out who did JB, you might avoid coming up dead yourself. Not entirely logical thinking, but thinking nonetheless. Did the police say anything about JB being shot?" He stood and turned around so he could urinate off the side of the building.

"No, said he drowned. Far as I know he hadn't been shot."

"Well, that's good. Probably wasn't me did it then." He'd been looking out at the boats negotiating the narrow channel, but glanced down, "Oops, sorry Moe." He took a step sideways. "So you want to know if JB planning to ban shark fishing would piss anyone off enough they'd want to kill the man?"

"Yeah, pretty much."

He did a little dance step, zipped, and sat back down. The man had the damnedest collection of scars on his hands and arms. He took a long pull on the pitcher to help him think.

"Might be some recreational fishermen getting their panties in a bunch, but that's about it. Ain't no commercial shark fishing around here, and if the ban had gone into effect, the weekend warriors could have just chartered with me."

Which didn't make sense. "But wouldn't the ban be putting you out of business?"

"Shit no! That was the whole idea of the ban. Nobody could catch sharks except for me and maybe a couple others. We'd be grandfathered in with a special license and have plenty of business. I'd just give ol' JB a kick on every charter. Damn shame the boy come up dead like that. Both of us stood to make a pile of money."

Chapter Thirteen

By the time I got away from Shark Hunter, it was late afternoon. He'd got into telling shark stories and bragging about recently coming into some really great chum for sharks but wouldn't tell me what it was. We did see one minor boat wreck in the channel. Two jet skis came blasting around boats, and one caught a wave and bounced pretty good off the side of a Bayliner, which proceeded to turn sharp and run aground just outside the channel. Plenty of angry yelling between the jet skis and the Bayliner until someone on the boat started casting a big topwater plug, trying for a hookup on one of the jet skiers.

There weren't any messages on my cellphone, so I assumed things were on track and we were still meeting at Pirate Jim's. Slip didn't have a cell but could have used a phone at the courthouse or newspaper. His problems with mechanical devices definitely included cellphones.

I decided to run by Julie's one more time. Everything there looked the same, no one around. The front door was locked so I went around to check the one in back. I stopped to try to look in a window just as a big cop came around the corner of the house.

"Sir, could I ask what you're doing?"

Oh, shit.

"Looking for a friend. She was supposed to call me this morning, but didn't."

"Could you come with me?"

As we went around front I could see a window curtain pulled back in the house across the street. Busted by a paranoid neighbor.

So I sat in the back of a police car while he called in to check me out.

"Taco Bob. This your correct address?" Holding my driver's license.

"Yes, sir."

"Report of a meth lab there recently."

I could see where this was going.

"Computer has you finding the body of the man who owns this house not long before that."

I hate computers.

"Yes sir. His sister has been staying here and she may be missing."

He gave me a glance from his paperwork. "When was she seen last?"

"Last night, I reckon."

"Who saw her and where?"

"I did, on my houseboat."

Another quick glance. I could almost see it register in his mind: drug related. After a few more minutes he let me out of the back of the patrol car.

"Mr. Bob, I would recommend that you stay off the premises."

This was accompanied by a stern cop look. I started to say something but decided to let it ride.

By the time I found a place to park, I was a half-hour late, and since I'm rarely late for anything, I expected to hear about it. But I didn't expect what I saw in Pirate Jim's.

At a table in the middle of the room, a young woman with snake hair, a gray face, bloody teeth and vacant eyes sat next to a man in an expensive suit and slicked-back hair. My friends had turned into a zombie and a lawyer. I couldn't decide which was worse.

"I just can't leave you two on your own for a minute, can I?"

I had a seat, and Consuelo grabbed my wrist and started gnawing and growling. Slip held a legal pad up to the light and was giving it his full concentration.

Thankfully, those two were the only things out of the ordinary in the place. There were a few tourists and locals and an older man at the bar in a threadbare shirt, wearing an old hat with a green parrot perched on top. He was talking to an attractive tourist woman and cleaning his toenails with a huge knife. I waved at Fish Daddy and he held up a finger to let me know he'd be over in a minute.

The zombie had gone from gentle gnawing to licking. I retrieved my arm.

"Mmmm …" Consuelo licked her lips.

"Looks like you found the voodoo lady. She do all this to you? Make you her voodoo slave?"

This got me a wide-eyed stare.

"No way! This brain-eater is a slave to no one! Well, could be to one person." A big wink before she lunged at me. She was growling away and trying to sink her plastic teeth into my arm when Fish Daddy came to the table with his constant companion perched on his hat.

"If y'all are busy I can come back later."

I had to admit, Consuelo was mighty attractive, even as a zombie. I removed her from my arm.

"Not at all. Little lady here is just a mite hungry. Maybe we should get her some chowder."

The mention of food brought Slip up from his notes as Fish Daddy took a seat at the table. I gave the dapper Slip a raised eyebrow about his apparel.

"Borrowed it from Jimmy. Thought it might make things go a bit easier."

"Did it?"

He just smiled and wiggled the legal pad.

The waitress appeared. I looked at our guest and he shook his head.

"Three bowls of your best chowder, ma'am."

Consuelo growled and cocked her head at the waitress.

"Do you have braaaaains?"

The waitress didn't miss a beat.

"No brains. Chowder."

She pointed at the pitcher of beer already on the table and looked at me. "Glass?"

"Yes, please. Fish?"

He pointed at his beer bottle and the waitress was gone. I did the intros.

"You know Slip, don't you?"

They shook across the table and both grunted something to the effect of hearing about the other.

"And under all the beads and makeup here is the fair lady Consuelo."

"Always a pleasure, my lady," he bowed slightly and Consuelo put down her beer and belched. They knew each other — Fish was a friend of her oldest sister.

"Taco, you remember the dreamer?" He pointed out the lean man with the short hair and uncertain eyes I'd seen before. The fella looked to be about mid-twenties, just sitting there by himself at a table close by, looking at his hands. He gave us a weak wave.

"Poor ol' boy still hasn't snapped out of it. Doesn't remember his name or nothing. Told me everything looks iridescent to him, like it does sometimes just before a big rain."

I gave my dressed-to-kill partners a quick rundown of the dreamer's story. Fish gave us the latest.

"I've been taking care of him, letting him stay at my place." Fish turned to me as the food arrived, "So, Taco, you said on the phone you thought maybe somebody whacked ol' JB the Manatee?"

I launched into telling him about Julie speculating that her brother's untimely demise might not have been an accident. Told him the same people could be planning on doing her and even us some harm. I was about to the part where JB wanted to step up bar inspections, when the bird crawled down the man who'd been known to enter the annual Hemingway Look-a-Like contest. The bright green parrot got on the table, then walked over in front of Consuelo, and tilted his head to give her a good look. The bird did a loud wolf whistle before talking.

"Nice tits!"

Consuelo had taken her plastic teeth out for the chowder. She smiled big and stuck her chest out at the bird.

"Why, how nice of you to notice, Captain Tom!"

The bird walked over toward Slip, gave him a long sideways look, then flew at his face. Slip and chair went over backwards and the bird landed on the floor. Fish grabbed up the bird and held him to his chest. Consuelo started laughing her head off, and Fish helped Slip get to his feet.

"I'm real sorry about that. That get-up you're wearing, he probably thought you were a lawyer."

Consuelo was about to gag from laughing. The bird went back up top and growled some at Slip.

Things finally settled down and we got back to it.

"Fish, we're leaning toward thinking it might have been one of JB's campaign promises that got him in trouble."

"By trouble, you mean dead and going out with the tide?"

"Pretty much, yeah. Among other things, he supposedly wanted to see the health department crack down on the bars."

"Oh, that's nothing. Just your typical politician smoke. Get the voters convinced something like more bar inspections is going to cure everything wrong in the city. Then if they swallow that and you get elected, just hire an extra inspector for a few weeks, then transfer 'em to another department where they can do you some good. They might not start out that way, but most all politicians end up worthless. Smart ones know good public relations people can cover for a world of screwing up. Smartest thing JB could have done as mayor would be hire a hot-shot PR student just out of school, let 'em work for the health department for a while, then turn 'em loose on damage control."

I was impressed, "You certainly seem to have a handle on all this."

"Well, I let JB buy me a few beers when he first started talking about this mayor thing."

A shapely young lady in a bikini top and shorts came by our table headed for the bar. The parrot leaned toward her as she got close, "Nice tits!"

The girl blushed and the boyfriend in tow gave the bird and all of us a dirty look. Fish handed up a sunflower seed and continued, "With my public image somewhat lacking at times, JB'd have to hire some suit to be his campaign manager." He looked at Slip. "No offense." Slip nodded. "And I'd likely have just been his behind-the-scenes advisor."

"That's mighty nice of you, help the man like that."

"Well, JB was a good fella, and that's just the kind of generous person I am." He smiled big just as some bird crap landed in his lap.

Consuelo clanged her spoon in the empty chowder bowl and pointed at Fish, "Don't you have a niece taking public relations classes in Miami? Or did she already graduate?"

Fish smiled and shrugged. This was getting interesting.

"So if you were advising JB, you probably know about the rest of his platform."

"I knew about it. Can't say I agreed with all his crazy ideas, though."

"You knew about banning shark fishing?"

"For everyone except that crazy fucker Clarence Hunter and a couple other charter captains. Simple kickback scheme."

Slip and Consuelo looked at me. I shrugged and nodded. Consuelo took it.

"What about JB wanting to rid the island of voodoo?"

"Mostly a favor for a woman has a shop over on Fleming. It was the only way she could get out of the iron-clad lease she was stuck with."

Consuelo leaned back in her chair and blew a loose strand of hair out of her eyes. "Yep, that's what I just spent all afternoon and seventy-five dollars for this crazy hairdo to find out."

We all mumbled something to the effect of how nice her hair looked.

"She told me while doing my hair that she was so upset when her old friend JB died, she stuck pins in his picture for leaving her with ten more years on the lease." Slip looked nervous.

"So I reckon you know about him wanting to go after developers."

Fish pulled out his big knife and went to work on his toenails. Being a gentleman, he'd waited until we all finished eating first.

"That's the part I didn't understand. Sure it's easy to kick developers. Anybody ever read one of those popular novels about Florida knows developers these days are about as welcome as a wet fart. But developers got something most all politicians need: cash. I told JB it didn't make any sense badmouthing those folks, even if they do tend to cause an ecological disaster here and there, deplete natural resources, and generally build tacky shit that if they aren't eyesores right off, will be sooner or later. I told the man, 'You want to go after developers or anybody for that matter, kiss some butt, get the campaign contributions so you can buy a few thousand little signs and overpriced TV and newspaper ads, get yourself elected, then go back and stab the developers in the back.' Man was hard-headed on that one issue, wouldn't listen to me." Fish Daddy held up a foot and leaned down and bit something, then spit before going back at it with the knife. We were finally getting somewhere.

"Sounds like he was about to step on some toes then. JB's sister said he was most upset at that developer who wants to build onto the island, like they did in Hong Kong for the new airport."

Fish acted like he couldn't be bothered to look up from his pedicure for such an absurd idea. "No way in God's Gray Earth they could ever get around the environmentalists to pull permits for something like that."

Slip cleared his throat and held his pad up. "Not only could, but did. The permits went through yesterday and they can start any time."

Chapter Fourteen

The Wilbur is not a particularly sleek, fast, or fancy boat, but it's sturdy and seaworthy. Built for cruising, it just takes a few wild ideas, way too much time and effort, and eventually you've got yourself a custom fishing boat with a gas oven so you can troll for dolphin and bake cookies at the same time. Consuelo brought some highly aromatic chocolate chips out on deck after letting them cool.

"Captain, care for a cookie?"

I put my laptop away and concentrated on the cookies. Not that I'd been getting much work done on my book anyway. Between keeping an eye on the trolling lines and inhaling the smell of cookies baking, my attention had been about maxed out. Even though I'd gotten to bed at a reasonable hour the night before, it must have been all the talk of murdered manatees and carrot peelers that gave me nightmares again.

I took my time selecting a tasty morsel from the tray, trying to ignore the pathetic whimpering noises coming from the flying bridge and the two tanned distractions partially wrapped in bikini cloth looming over the cookies.

"These taste half as good as they smell …," I couldn't make up my mind, so I took four. Our lovely cook flipped one over her shoulder in the direction of the helm.

"Incoming!"

I glanced up to see Slip with the cookie sticking out of his mouth and his full attention back on the cookie tray.

"Eyes on the road, helmsman! We don't want any accidents this morning."

Consuelo flipped up another cookie. Her hair back to its usual page-boy, sans bead snakes.

"Aye, aye, captain!"

It was hot, with hardly a breath of breeze, so I didn't say anything about the lady's skimpy attire. Slip and I were down to just shorts and I didn't want to get into another debate about her wanting to do the same. She set the tray in the galley and leaned against the fighting chair where I was sitting.

"These are good Consuelo, very tasty." I was rat-nibbling, trying to make them last, they were so damn good.

"Yeah, I'm getting used to that oven finally. I'm thinking pie next trip. You like lemon meringue or pumpkin?"

One of the reels started clicking, but slowly. Consuelo went for it and started reeling in to clear the line.

"Grass!"

Which was all that seemed to be biting. I was about to say it anyway, when Slip called down.

"TB, you said if we weren't doing anything by the time the cookies were done."

"Yep. Let's get the lines in and head for the hills."

We were still several miles out from the marina when Slip yelled and pointed. Consuelo came out of the galley and I stowed the laptop. The seas were calm enough that I could get a good look with the glasses while the old Wilbur lumbered along at her cruising speed of seventeen knots.

"Looks like barges. Several big ones with a full load of something." There wasn't much doubt in my mind as I handed the big military binoculars to Consuelo. She confirmed it.

"Sand. Barges loaded with sand. Eight, no, nine of them coming from the east."

We changed course for the southern side of Key West. The shallow flats, where on a normal day you might see the occasional fishing boat, jet ski, or wind surfer, were filled with boats of all sizes and shapes. There were more barges, all pushed by giant tugboats, some already empty and heading back for another load. Two barges filled with heavy equipment and cranes were close to the sand barges being unloaded by more machines that looked like big yellow bugs from a distance. Several dozen boats were in the area, some of them workboats, some gawkers. Slip cut back on the engines and we prepared to do some gawking ourselves. Up top, Slip had the best view.

"Busy little beavers, aren't they?"

We joined him for a better look.

"I reckon. They sure aren't wasting any time."

Consuelo had the big glasses on the situation. I was surprised at the scene, to say the least.

"This is a big deal. How did they coordinate all this without anyone knowing? The logistics of this are incredible."

Slip cleared his throat and went into what we now referred to as his lawyer mode. "I told y'all yesterday at Pirate Jim's I thought there was more going on than what the media said. Some of those people I talked to at the courthouse and newspaper were acting a mite cagey."

We were moving slow, getting closer to the action. Something of this magnitude, there were going to be a few problems. Near one of the barges unloading we could see the top half of a bulldozer sticking up out of the shallow water with a slick of diesel fuel spreading around it. Several workers stood on the barge with hands on their hips looking down. A man in the water next to the dozer was trying to hook up a cable from one of the big cranes.

There was a sign on a post in the water ahead of us and more signs forming a line in each direction.

"What's it say, Consuelo?"

"'Keep Out — Marine Research Area.' At the bottom, 'Have A Nice Day — Blue Manatee, Inc.'"

A good-size mullet skiff was deploying what looked like a net along the row of signs that seemed to go as far as you could see around the area. I realized what the net had to be.

"Silt screen. Though I can't see how that's going to do much good for the mess they're making."

Consuelo snapped her fingers twice to signal danger, "Bogey, three o'clock."

A speedboat inside the construction area slowed just before it got to us. We went to full stop about fifty feet from the nearest sign. The speedboat came up next to the sign, and a big burly sort pointed at the sign and smiled a menacing smile. We gave the smile back and he glared at us a few seconds. He finally pulled away, going back to his patrol. Held his arm up so we could see the gun under his tropical shirt. I noticed Consuelo was airing her middle finger and didn't look too happy.

"Did that jerk's shirt have blue manatees on it?"

Slip took the glasses for a look.

"Probably. That's the name on most of the permits I saw yesterday. Had a Miami address." He put the glasses down. "Gives you a nice feeling, doesn't it? Like any company with a name like Blue Manatee wouldn't do anything bad."

We answered the man with disbelieving grunts as we continued to look over the area. Slip turned the boat and we moved along slowly just outside the signs. Two powerboats were setting orange posts. I pointed.

"Surveyors?"

Slip had the glasses again.

"Looks like it. Probably local. I think I've seen one of those guys around."

I was still wondering where everyone else came from, not to mention the equipment.

"They must have had a staging area for all this. The upper Keys or Miami. Or maybe even some from the Bahamas. We know from the newspaper that they were talking about getting fill from a sandspit island in the Bahamas. Someone had to be putting this together for months. They got lucky with the weather right when the permits went through." Then there was still the big question. "I'd like to know who's behind Blue Manatee. Has to be someone with incredible amounts of money, power, and influence."

Slip gave my arm a nudge. "You mean someone like Jimmy Buffett, or maybe Carl Hiaasen?"

Consuelo slapped him on the shoulder. "No, smart ass. It's probably some huge company like MegaDrug. I could see those bastards doing something like this."

When we got back to *Sandy Bottomed Girl*, I'd been feeling a case of the carefuls coming on, so I took a quick look around.

"The door was still locked and I don't think anyone has been in here."

I had a seat on the couch, and Slip dropped in a chair where he could see anyone coming down the dock. Consuelo still hadn't said much. She went in the galley and started banging pots and pans.

"Consuelo! Could you lay off the cookware?"

There were a couple more clangs, then quiet. She came in and sat frowning on the other end of the couch. "Sorry. I shouldn't let people like that Blue Manatee redneck upset me. What are we going to do?"

"I want to go by Julie's again, then check Smathers Beach. Looked like something going on there. We start with that?" Nods. "And we better stick together, watch each other's back for a while. Might be a good idea if we could figure a way to blend in a little more, just in case someone is looking for us."

"Totally. I need to call my sisters at the hotel anyway."

Slip looked uncomfortable. "Taco, I'm going to use the bathroom, get cleaned up some."

I wondered if getting cleaned up was becoming a trend for the man. I looked over at Consuelo to see if I'd heard right. She just shrugged.

Consuelo's sister Lydia came by with a bag of clothes, and the two women disappeared in the direction of the guest stateroom. Slip, all showered and wearing clothes I lent him, sat with me in the lounge. I'd cleaned up and changed as well. We were both wearing baggy tourist outfits topped with ball caps, ready to walk out the door, just waiting for the ladies. I decided to take a quick look on the net, see what a search for Blue Manatee might bring up. Slip started pacing as I flipped on my laptop.

"Taco, Consuelo told me not to tell you this, but under the circumstances —"

The phone rang, I answered. It was Mary Ann wanting to talk about her job. I told her I had a lot going on, was about to leave. She asked who with. I told her and she said we needed to talk about my friends. She started to say something else but Lydia came into the room. I said I really have to go, can I call you later when I get back, and she hung up. I turned the computer off and stowed it away. That would have to wait until we got back.

Consuelo came in next, but it wasn't her. Brown wig, too much makeup, dark glasses, and a baggy tropical shirt and hat to match. Perfect.

"Very nice, Lydia. I can't hardly tell it's her."

Consuelo smiled shyly and belched. Slip rolled his eyes.

"It's her. Let's roll."

Chapter Fifteen

We dropped Lydia at the hotel so we could use the car. Not that a big, rusty convertible with a sunrise painted on the hood and sunset on the trunk was all that anonymous, but it was a little less conspicuous than my truck with the homemade camper on back.

I explained why I should stay in the car on our way to check on Julie. I didn't want any conversations with the police as to why I was back. But still no sign of Julie, and I wasn't sorry to see the house across the street had a moving van parked out front. Consuelo drove.

"Taco, I'm worried about her. You told the cop she was missing?"

"Yep, not that he seemed too receptive to anything I had to say. Maybe when we get back to my place we'll try calling in a missing person. Can't hurt."

Smathers Beach was just around the corner. A section on the west end fenced off a large gazebo, landscaping, colorful signs, and a fair throng of people that I didn't remember being there before.

"I'll drop you guys here and find a place to park this beast."

Slip and I jumped out and eased up on the throng. Workers were finishing up a last section of paving bricks, but the rest of the area seemed to be done. A small park had sprung up overnight, complete with someone in the gazebo, holding a microphone, wrapping up a speech about environmental centers and bringing affordable housing to Key West. The barges and equipment out on the water were a backdrop seen through numerous freshly planted palms.

We merged with the crowd, checking out the signs depicting happy street scenes of the coming development. There were several of the big, full-color signs along the paver walkways surrounded by lush plants and palms. Each sign had a different idyllic scene with the words "Affordable Housing" and "Environmentally Friendly" at the bottom and a picture of a blue manatee.

"Taco, this is mighty nice."

"Yeah, these people are good at this. Got themselves some world-class propaganda going on here."

The crowd was eating it up. At least the tourists were, some of the locals didn't look too happy. I saw a couple of people I vaguely knew having words with the man who'd been making the speech and a few others in the gazebo. One of those noticed me about the same time I realized who he was.

"Slip, look who we got rubbing elbows with these people."

"Well, look at that. You ever ask him about those calls to the police?"

"Tried to. Saw him heading down the dock and ran over to talk but he told me he didn't have time for hippie cowboy lowlifes."

Slip looked genuinely surprised. "He said that?"

"His very words. I tried again, but he went on aboard his fancy boat ignoring me. I reckon some people are just assholes."

Slip was staring toward the gazebo. "I'll say. Man's got the social graces of a sea slug."

Grizzel kept glancing over toward a big goon standing in the shade of a palm. I looked around and saw several more of the same lurking along the edges of the park. One taking pictures of the crowd, others talking on walkie-talkies.

"Slip, they got a lot of muscle here."

"Yeah, I noticed," Slip took a few pictures with the camera he'd brought to go with his outfit. "I think this thing is broken."

"It is. You don't think I'd loan you a working digital camera, do you?"

"Yeah, good point."

Someone on the gazebo started handing out free t-shirts, and the crowd surged that way.

"Slip, we need to stick together. I wish Consuelo would get here."

"You don't need to worry about her. Like I started to tell you —"

"There she is."

I could see flashes of her lime green hat bobbing through the crowd. She had someone in tow.

"Hey guys! Look who I found!" It was the dreamer, looking as dazed as ever.

"Found him sitting on the curb. I think he wandered off and ended up here." The man gave me a shrug. "We should call Fish. Do you have his cell number?"

"Yeah, it's in my wallet. Give me a minute and I'll see if I can dig it out."

Consuelo gave the place a look. "This is impressive. Says here the environment is the first concern and every effort is made to work in harmony with nature. Where's the part about killing politicians dressed like manatees? Is that around on back?" She stepped off the path into the plantings and looked at the back of the sign. "Nope, nothing about killing people back here."

Slip snapped his fingers twice.

"Two o'clock. One in front, two behind."

Three big guys in matching blue shirts rolled up on us.

"Ma'am, could you step out of the landscaping, please?"

He pointed to a little sign, "Please Stay on Pathways." Consuelo looked up from under her wide-brim hat and popped her gum.

"Hey, no problem!" She jumped to my side and put her arms around my waist, head against my shoulder. "Honey, can we go get a margarita now? You promised!"

The security guy ignored Consuelo's performance, but you could see a look of recognition on his face when he noticed the dreamer standing behind Slip. The big goon started talking low into his walkie-talkie and the dreamer started fidgeting, then stepping backwards. Time to go.

The dreamer turned and ran, Consuelo right behind, and Slip and I bringing up the rear. She caught him pretty quick and had him down to a fast walk in the direction of the car. We could hear him mumbling, scared. I looked back.

"They're not following us. I suggest we leave before they change their minds."

We forced the dreamer and ourselves to walk calmly the rest of the way to the car. The top still down.

"Nice and easy, Consuelo."

She drove normally, except for looking in the rearview mirror every five seconds. I called Fish Daddy.

"Fish? We got your boy. ... Yeah, the dreamer. ... Sure, no problem. We're going there now. ... See you then."

Slip sat in back, trying not to look behind us, the dreamer next to him, crouched down on the floor.

"Fish has been out looking for him, said he'd come by and collect him later."

Consuelo kept looking in the mirror.

"We got a tail. Two guys in a blue pickup. Don't turn around."

I looked in the side mirror. They were closing.

"They're trying to get close enough to get the tag. Hold on."

Hard enough right turn the big car squealed the tires a little. Then another right and we were back on Roosevelt Boulevard, the beach flying by on the left. Consuelo's hands at ten after ten on the wheel, deftly weaving through traffic. A right down a narrow street, then cut through a parking lot and come out on Flagler. No sign of the blue pickup in my mirror.

"I think you lost 'em."

"Yeah, I always wanted to do that."

Slip gave her a pat on the back, "Nice work. Remind me to buy you a beer."

Driving with traffic now, taking the side streets back to the marina on the other side of the island.

"Someone's been here."

Slip and Consuelo froze behind me as I stepped inside the houseboat.

"Couch looks a bit too neat."

We spread out and took a thorough look around. A few things were not quite in the right place. I took a closer look at the door.

"Must have used a lock-pick of some kind. Guess I'll start setting the alarm."

Slip was checking out the bedrooms.

"Do you think they were looking for your book?"

"No telling, but I wouldn't be surprised." I took my laptop out of the old boat's secret hidey-hole and set it on the table in the lounge. I fired up the computer. Consuelo came out of the galley with three cold beers.

"Try Blue Manatee. They probably have a Web site to match their cute little expo-park I bet." Consuelo and Slip were looking over my shoulder.

They did. Page after page of a top-notch Web site, long on alluding to how Southernmost Community — the new development's name — would solve all of Key West's problems by providing housing for the service sector. They were definitely saying all the right things, since it's true that Key West waiters and store clerks often had to work two jobs just to make their share of the rent for old house trailers on tiny weedy lots on Stock Island, the next island up the Keys. Those moldy trailers and lots were selling for about the same as new homes in the nicer subdivisions on the mainland.

The only other cheap housing option isn't even a house, or on land. Just off Stock Island there's a growing community of derelict boats spread out and anchored up over several acres of water. Boats that folks can rent or buy to live on. Besides most being pretty uncomfortable from not having air-conditioning or even electricity, the little boats catch hell from hurricanes, which is probably the only reason Key West doesn't have the biggest floating slum in the U.S.

The Blue Manatee Web site boasted forty reasonably priced units available on completion of Phase I. Consuelo pointed to an artist's rendition of jolly bartenders, t-shirt shop clerks, and museum guides playing volleyball on the beach with their affordable housing in the background. "Probably a crumb thrown to the planning board so they can make the rest of the project gated, high-end condos."

She was likely right, since plans for the rest of the project were vague at best. Most of the site was pictures of children playing with kittens and retirees strolling along beaches with porpoises frolicking in the background. I felt the houseboat move, then a knock. Fish Daddy.

"Damned if I know what to do with him, figured he'd been snapped out of it by now. I was going to ask Consuelo's sisters and you folks if you had any ideas. I hate to turn him over to the police."

We all sat around the lounge watching the man with the parrot on his hat pace back and forth. The dreamer sat in a corner on the floor, vaguely aware of everyone looking at him. We'd told Fish about how the security goons had scared him.

Slip cleared his throat. "We could sell him to the voodoo lady. She could make him into a zombie. Wouldn't take much the way he is now."

We all gave Slip a look for his crappy joke, except Consuelo.

"Hey, Cro-Magnon man here might have something. I think Miss Levita said something about being a licensed hypnotist when she did my hair. Maybe she could do something for him."

"Consuelo, I think that license —"

Fish cut me off, "Hey, that's an idea! A damn good idea!" He went over and got the dreamer on his feet. "I'll take him over there right now! Don't know why I didn't think of that!" And they were out the door, Fish still talking and the bird holding on. Next order of business: Julie.

"Consuelo, given the lack of enthusiasm I got from the police last time, maybe you could give them a call, mention Julie is missing?"

"Not that I'm likely on their Christmas card list either, but I'll give it a shot." She headed for the phone. I'd been meaning to ask.

"Which reminds me. What was that all about, anyway? I never did hear the whole story."

"Oh, nothing really. Some guy kind of bumped into me and fell on a cop. They dropped the charges, just a misunderstanding."

Most likely, since she sure didn't look very dangerous with that smile. Then again, Slip had mentioned something once about her knowing karate. Hard to believe with her sitting there talking on the phone, looking up at me like that.

"Earth to Taco! Come in, Taco!" Slip being cute.

"What?" I yawned. I really needed a night without crazy dreams.

"I'm going to take a walk, stretch my legs."

"Be careful."

Chapter Sixteen

My body had molded itself into the fibers of the beach hammock, the only sound the gentle murmur of the sea and an occasional bird squawking in the distance. I felt so comfortable, so at peace. Realizing I'd been sleeping on my arm, I moved it ever so carefully so I could go back to sleep. The hammock swayed slightly, a seagull screamed closer, I sighed and started drifting again into the comforting arms of sleep. The hammock moved again. I opened my eyes, realizing this time I was really awake, lying on the old yellow couch. My internal alarm had gone off, meaning someone had just come aboard.

With all my senses racing toward full alert, I lifted my head enough to look across the dark lounge. The only light came from my small portable television across the room. The picture frozen showing a close-up of a man with the handle of a kitchen implement sticking out of his bloody forehead. My two acquaintances also frozen, sitting on the floor looking back my way, their eyes as big as dinner plates. A nearly empty bowl of popcorn on the floor between them. Slip holding the VCR remote.

I held up one finger, but Consuelo was already moving low across the room, coming up between the window and the door. I motioned for Slip to move slow, then sat up and eased to the other side of the door. My right arm hanging by my side.

Consuelo peeked through the window curtain, showed us with one hand: a male, medium height, coming toward the door. She stood slightly crouched, but looked relaxed, her eyes hooded. A second later, a tentative soft knock.

"Hello? Anyone home?"

I tried shaking my numb arm a little. "Who's there?"

"Danny, Danny Morgan."

I looked and got shrugs from my cohorts. Slip was next to me holding the remote in a menacing way. I guess he couldn't find the heavy flashlight.

"Oh, sorry. I was here earlier? You brought me in the big car?"

I opened the door a crack, then pulled him in and stuck my head out the door for a quick look. All clear. I looked at my watch for the first time after closing the door. Nearly midnight.

"Sorry about coming by so late. I just wanted to thank you for helping me."

Consuelo got up close to him, looking in his eyes.

"You saw Levita? She fixed you?"

"Yes! She's great! I owe her big!"

Consuelo went back to her seat next to the popcorn.

"Well, at least he's talking."

"Oh, I could talk before. But I was busy with, you know, other things."

I motioned for him to have a seat. "Fish said you were lucid dreaming, got stuck or something."

"Yeah, grabbed one of those scouts. Guess I'll think twice before I do that again!" He was the only one laughing.

Slip went back to the television, started rewinding the tape in the VCR, looking for something.

"So you were lucid dreaming. What do you mean you could talk, but were busy?"

His expression changed — serious now. "I mostly knew what was going on around me, in this plane." Motions to indicate the here and now. "But I got involved in reading my past. There's kind of like a permanent record stored in our DNA. Fascinating stuff. I was able to watch any part of my life, like watching a movie." Looks from the floor by the television. "I thought it was only for a few hours, but I guess it was more like several days." Ownership of the VCR remote became more important on the other side of the room, but I was interested.

"See any good stuff on your DNA movie? Like why you were afraid of those guys at the park?"

"Yeah, I'll say. That one guy, he works for DDT."

"Which is?"

"DDT? Big time money behind Blue Manatee. When I was surfing my DNA, I could collate bits and pieces of things from my past experiences. Like, I never realized that guy worked for DDT and he didn't really care about the environmental movement."

"You're losing me here."

"Sorry. You see, I'm vice president of the Beach Animal Research Foundation." Looked like he was proud of this. "You've heard of us?"

"BARF? Uh, well."

"We're part of a coalition of environmental groups that monitor coastal development. It's kind of a shock to realize now that a lot of the members of those groups actually work for DDT. They must have been planting people for years. One of those guys at the gazebo is president of CRABS. Too bad too, he always had some great drugs at the environmental conferences."

The fella sat there with a big goofy grin. I got a quick eye roll from Slip that told me what he thought and Consuelo scratched the side of her head and let her finger do one circle around her ear. They went back to their movie.

But if Danny was right, it would go a long way toward explaining why the local environmentalists, who could at times go into a frenzy over something like what kind of mulch the county used, would let something of this magnitude go down.

"Care for something to drink?"

'Oh, no! I just wanted to thank you for everything. I really need to get back. Miss Levita is waiting for me. Said she'd have a big surprise waiting."

The next morning I woke in my bed after another restless night of bad dreams. At least I'd gotten a little sound sleep on the couch before our late night visitor. Since we'd decided to stick close for a few days, Slip had spent the night on the couch, Consuelo the guest quarters. Just after I'd heard Slip start to snore someone tried my bedroom doorknob. The lock held.

The next morning a somewhat grumpy Consuelo offered to make breakfast, and I decided to check out DDT. A search of DDT on the net produced no Web site or any way to confirm that the organization really existed but plenty of information on insecticides, wrestling, and debugging. There were, however, numerous conspiracy sites filled with wild speculation blaming DDT — the unholy alliance of dentists, dermatologists, and teamsters — for everything from bird flu to rising gasoline prices to the JFK assassination. There were also pages showing financial estimations and projections for DDT. The figures varied greatly, but most seemed to point to the Florida dermatologists as having the highest revenue and being the real force behind DDT. One blog referred to them as "a shocking example of excessive greed and the abuse of trust." Another compared their billing practices to "being sexually assaulted with a blowtorch."

"Nice people, those DDT," Slip hovered over me looking at the screen.

"Well, at least Danny didn't make that up."

Consuelo came in the room and handed me a steaming cup of coffee, then checked the Web page on my laptop. Slip headed for the galley and the coffee. While I took a sip of coffee, she reached over my shoulder to click a link and give me a soft spearing in the back of the head.

"Jeez, TB, some great endorsements here. Look at this whistle-blower site: 'DDT's revenues make Fort Knox look like a piggy bank,' and 'The most ruthless bastards since the Huns vacationed in Rome.' This from a guy who says he's a dermatologist who got kicked out for not charging enough. Says he's in hiding and fears for his life."

"Well, if Blue Manatee really is backed by DDT, then it sure sounds like the kind of folks who wouldn't let a small-time politician get in the way." Or his sister. "After breakfast, why don't you call our friends down at the police station again, see if they've located Julie."

"'Kay. Scrambled with green chilies, grits, bacon, ham, sausage links, hash browns, biscuits, red-eye gravy, goat cheese, sliced tomatoes, orange juice, and Key Lime pie sound okay?"

"Scrambled sounds great. But speaking on behalf of my digestive system, I think I'll pass on the chilies. Don't want to overdo it."

After being on hold for fifteen minutes, Consuelo learned from the police that they didn't have any news on Julie. When asked if they'd checked her brother's house lately, they said they couldn't, so that's where we went first.

It wasn't exactly first thing, though. We needed new disguises. Before we left the marina, Slip and I borrowed some country-club slacks and sport shirts from Jimmy Redd. Told him we were going to play a joke on someone. Good thing we were all about the same size.

We eased out to the car, keeping an eye out for anyone or anything suspicious. So far, so good. First stop, the airport for a rental after being tailed the day before.

After the clothes and car, a stop at the hotel. Twenty minutes later she came out as a he, dressed like us and even a pencil-thin mustache. We must have looked pretty shocked. Consuelo said it was a hobby of her sisters'.

When we got to JB's place, we found out why the police couldn't check on the house — it was gone. Just a vacant lot fast becoming part of a causeway going out to what had become a small island of barged sand. Dump trucks, bulldozers, front-end loaders, and road graders all in motion and making a hell of a racket.

The house across the street now a construction office. Most of the foliage stripped away, with trucks and heavy equipment parked in the yard. Several workers putting up a chain-link fence around the property. We just stared for a few seconds. Slip broke the silence.

"Holy Jumping Jesus! These people work fast!"

Our driver saw the man first. "Watcher on the back roof of the construction office."

I motioned for her to turn the car around.

"Good call, Consuelo. He's probably a spotter for the dispatcher and security. We look too interested he'll have someone on us."

As we left another car full of eyes came down the street to take our place.

A drive-by on the new park proved interesting enough for a closer look. Got lucky with a metered spot right on the boulevard a couple hundred yards down from the park. I put in some coins.

"Might be wise to split up this time. You got your phone?" Consuelo held up a pink flip-phone. "Slip, why don't you two give me a minute or so. Let me take point." The little guy standing next to Slip started to protest, but settled for a frown.

I made my way along the sidewalk through the strollers, skaters, and joggers. An occupied blue pickup parked up ahead looked like a good reason to take the scenic route along the beach for a ways.

The big signs in the park were all painted solid green — the reason we wanted a closer look. Behind me, Slip coming the same way along the beach. Consuelo walking down the sidewalk so she could get a look at the pickup truck.

The signs painted over were about the only difference. Another good crowd to hide in and another speaker in the gazebo. Politician going on about the great things going on here — jobs, affordable housing. No Grizzel this time.

I thought about what Danny had said. If DDT would spend years planting their people in the environmental groups, they'd most likely be doing the same thing with the politicians. I couldn't begin to imagine what several acres of raw land in Key West was worth, but there was only so much shallow in that area that they could fill before the bottom dropped off. Seemed like a lot of trouble. Maybe the DDT planned to build a big hotel and convention center just for dentists and dermatologists. I could imagine why they joined with the teamsters, an outfit with a troubled financial past but capable of a lot of heavy lifting. There were several big stereotypical examples of teamsters lurking again today, watching the crowd. I tried to hide behind my Panama hat as much as I could.

"New in town, big fella?" Consuelo playing gay guy, waving a cigarette, needing a light.

"Yeah, first time." I patted my pockets, looking around the park. "I'm looking for my wife." Came up with a lighter.

"I bet you are." Holding my wrist as the cigarette lit. "Maybe we should look for her together."

Slip had a conversation going with a big woman in an orange floral dress close to the gazebo. I pointed at the barges and equipment out beyond the palms.

"These people have got this down to the last detail. Hard to believe it's tooth pullers and skin carvers put this together. Amazing what enough money will do."

Consuelo wasn't paying attention, instead, holding her cigarette with her arm cocked and giving one of the big green signs a close appraisal. "It's just not as good as his earlier work, don't you agree, darling? I mean, it's green, but —"

A blast of loud music as a four-piece band took over for the politician. Slip looked away from the woman and nodded to let us know he had what we'd come to find out. A man with a big box started walking through the crowd handing out t-shirts and cozies. Some shoving. Time to go. Consuelo waited for Slip, and I started back to the car. I took about two steps and someone bumped me and forced something into my hand. Just saw the back of his head going through the crowd. I looked for Slip. He was going toward the little guy with the cigarette, giving me a questioning glance. I started for the car again, taking a peek at the handwritten note, "Scorpion Pit — 9 tonight bring your friend — JB is okay."

"So JB is feeling better? After being dead and decomposing in the gulf for a few days before we found him?"

Slip seemed most upset about the note when I read it aloud back in the car. Consuelo again driving smooth as silk, gave her report.

"I couldn't get much of a look in the truck — tinted windows. Had the engine running with the a/c on. Looked like one big guy, probably one of the security creeps." Checking the mirror again.

"I'd sure like to know who passed me this note." I hate surprises. "Slip, what did you find out about those signs?"

"That was Miss Agnes, lady I talked to before at the courthouse. She's about the only one I got much help from. I think she kind of likes me."

I turned around to look at Slip lying in the backseat with his feet propped up, smiling.

"She used to be a kindergarten teacher in Marathon, you know."

"The signs?"

"Yeah. Vandals wrote on 'em with spray paint last night. 'LIES!' 'MURDERERS!' Stuff like that. Someone trying to get the word out, I guess. The security people painted over the graffiti right away this morning. I seen some artists setting up when we were leaving. Bet the signs are back like they were by tomorrow."

I wouldn't doubt it. I also doubted Blue Manatee would leave the park another night without a watchman. At least there didn't seem to be much doubt about who took out JB and why.

"Between JB's plan to shut down Blue Manatee if he got elected mayor and him owning a key piece of real estate for the road to the new development, I'd say it's a lock DDT was the ones did him in. All we have to do is find the proof and turn it over to the cops."

The looks I got there in the convertible pretty much confirmed my own suspicions that finding the proof wouldn't be easy. We'd just have to keep our eyes open and come up with some kind of plan.

"Hey, Taco! Miss Agnes told me something else. She said one of the Martys in town wrote a song about Blue Manatee ruining Key West with that development. Supposed to be a pretty good song, maybe good enough to get on the radio."

"Good. Bet Blue Manatee wasn't expecting that."

Our driver gave a thumbs-up to show she agreed.

"Consuelo, stop by the grocery so we can pick up a few things. We can go back to my place, hole up there for a few hours. Then we'll go by the Scorpion Pit if a safer and saner idea doesn't present itself."

Chapter Seventeen

I was nodding by the time we got to the marina. We almost didn't see the blue pickup parked behind an RV. Our sharp-eyed driver picked out the two guys sitting there in the middle of the parking lot, reading a newspaper like it's the most common thing in the world for two guys to do in the tropics. That woke me up.

"They've got a clear view of the *Sandy Bottomed* all right. May as well just ignore them, stroll on inside. See what."

I grabbed a bag of groceries and my cohorts followed with the rest, whispering to each other. We dropped the groceries in the galley and watched the two men watching us for a while. I finally went in and started putting things away. Slip stayed on surveillance, Consuelo came and shooed me out of the galley.

"Let me do that, you take a nap. I'll get a stew going so it'll be ready when you wake up."

It's always been hard for me to argue with any kind of sound logic that involves sleep and food.

I was in a huge room. In the middle of the room, a bed, surrounded by some kind of guards. The foggy haze of the room mixing with a strong feeling of danger. I woke when the phone rang.

Mary Ann wanted to know what I was doing. I was having some trouble waking up and realized Slip and Consuelo were gone. I started a quick look through the houseboat but only found some stew simmering on the stove. I asked Mary Ann if I could call her right back and she asked why, so I told her. She started in on my friends again just as the boat moved and a second later they came strolling in wearing their regular clothes — big innocent smiles as soon as they saw me. I took the phone back in the bedroom for some privacy. I could hear activity in the kitchen and Slip saying something to Consuelo about being careful.

Mary Ann sounded different. I asked if there was something wrong and she said no, then, well, yes. The love of my life told me she didn't think this long-distance relationship was working out and anyway she'd been kind of seeing this guy from work. I'd like him. I told her I kinda doubted it under the circumstances. She said something about my friends and her friends. I asked her if we could just step back and think about this a little and I could call her back. She said it would be better if I didn't and hung up. After a minute or so of listening to the dial tone, I put the phone down and went in the bathroom and washed my face. At least the stew smelled good.

"What happened to *you?*"

Slip and Consuelo were in the kitchen, Slip holding his hand over the sink for Consuelo to bandage. All happy smiles again as soon as they saw me.

"Nothing. Fell on the gravel. They don't call me Slip for nothing!"

Both laughing, glancing to see if I was buying it.

"That pickup still out there?"

Slip had to think about it a second. "Uh, no. As a matter of fact, I think they left."

Consuelo kind of shrugging and nodding, done with nurse work and stirring the stew.

"Did you happen to talk to them before they left?" Conspiratorial looks at each other and more shrugging. "You two want to go ahead and tell me what happened so we can eat?" I checked my watch.

"Well, it was Blondie's idea" — a hard look from the cook — "and mine."

I went into the lounge and took a careful look outside. The truck was indeed gone. Consuelo came out and plopped in a chair.

"We just wanted to have a little talk. Find out why they were watching us. See if they knew anything about someone getting in here before."

I sat on the couch, and Slip came in and paced.

"That's right, she's the one with the questions, I just wanted to say hi."

Consuelo snorted, then picked it up. "Yeah, we walked up to the truck and said hi to one of the meatballs. The guy tells us to piss off and flips a lit cigarette at me. Bounced off my shorts. Chuck Norris here picks the butt up and goes over to the guy and says, 'You drop this?' then starts punching the shit out of him. The other one jumps out and runs around like he's going to start in on Slip so I tripped him a little."

I don't think she realized she was rubbing her callused knuckles while talking.

"Slip drags the first one out of the truck onto the ground, still punching him in the face. I kind of kicked the other guy some so he'd stay put. I didn't want him to get in the way and get hurt while Slip continued to get to know the first one."

"Yeah, I asked him what the fuck a few times, until he finally got tired of my fist on his face and said they were just supposed to keep an eye on the houseboat and call in any activity."

Consuelo let loose a little girl laugh. "Yeah, Rambo asks the guy, 'You mean this kind of activity?' and starts kicking the hell out of the other guy asking him what else. I got to admit, Slip had me about to bust a gut laughing."

All I could think was hopefully no one saw somebody beating the tar out of two big goons with a little blond standing there laughing.

"The guy finally got tired of my boot in his ribs and said they only did surveillance and thought maybe an enforcement crew would stop by later. We still had a few more questions, but some tourists were coming down the walk, so we helped the boys back in their truck. I guess they decided to call it a day."

More shrugs and innocent smiles.

"Enforcement, huh? Sounds like fun. I guess that'll give us something to look forward to later on after our visit to the Scorpion Pit."

On the way over I was still a bit in shock about Mary Ann. I just hadn't seen it coming. A lot of questions popped up in my mind, most of them concerned the guy she'd been seeing from work. They were not pretty thoughts.

We had to pull off the narrow road going into the Scorpion Pit for a cop car coming out, followed by an ambulance with its lights flashing. You could hear the place before you could see it. Actually, it wasn't the loud music and loud voices coming from the bar, all that was drowned out by the droning of dozens of big motorcycles jamming the parking lot. I remembered seeing in the paper it was Bike Week, one of several each year. This one was called Dirty Bike Week, an event with a history of appealing mostly to the lower crust of the biker barrel.

Parking back a ways with the car pointed toward the exit seemed like a good idea. The evening's wardrobe: construction-worker clothes and boots for the three of us. We walked to the building trying not to seem too curious about any of the murmurings, grunts, or shrieks going on in and around the parked cars and trucks in the dark lot.

"Maybe we should kind of hang outside a minute or two, see if our note man makes an appearance."

My partners agreed. We slowed our pace toward the front door. One streetlight shone over rows of bikes parked close, more bikes chugging through the lot making noise.

Two big scooter trash with shaved heads and bloody faces were trading punches at the edge of the light. Looked like they'd been at it awhile and were tiring, having trouble standing. No one paying any attention to them.

Closer to the door, three hot young women in biker gear stood together, smoking cigarettes, looking bored, and practicing their hard looks on us.

"Hey! Hey, over here!"

A little round guy in the shadows waving us over. We spread out some, eased his way.

"You're Taco Bob, right?" Young guy with a full head of dark hair wearing new cargo shorts and a knit shirt looking out of place but not particularly nervous.

"And you are?"

He seemed to be alone.

"Shawn Pooch. Can we talk?" He looked behind me. "Alone?"

"Under the circumstances, I think we'll all just stay close."

He shrugged and took a couple steps further back in the shadows, all of us looking around. The walls of the bar close, vibrating from the music inside. Rumbling motorcycles around us, yells and laughter from the roof.

"I don't know if you've heard of me, but I used to work for the newspaper here?"

I shook my head.

"Anyway, I did a story on the big development a few weeks ago."

I nodded now.

"Okay, so I was doing more research for another article when I got an offer from a newspaper up north. Kind of offer I couldn't refuse, if you know what I mean." Looking around again. "So I went to New Jersey, took the job up there doing obits, but kept up my research on the sly. As soon as they were convinced I was going to be a good boy I told them my mother was sick and I needed time off. I came back to the Keys instead." More looking around, then staring into my eyes.

"I want to stop Blue Manatee and I need your help. I don't want to tell you too much and put you in danger, but what they're doing is the beginning of the end for Key West. The people behind Blue Manatee will stop at nothing to get this project completed." Looking pretty angry now. "But like I said, I don't want to say too much in case you're captured and tortured." Always a pleasant thought.

"Uh-huh. Well my friends here have been trying to convince me that since we're the one's found JB's body, we're already likely on DDT's shit list. They've had some of their goons watching us, so you might say we're pretty much involved already."

He jumped just a little when I said DDT. I wanted to ask about the mention of JB in the note, but he didn't give me a chance.

"So you know about DDT?" His hand went to his goatee while he gave that some thought. "Well, DDT isn't the whole story, there's more." But it didn't look like he was going to say.

"So, you want us to help do what? No, wait. Don't tell me. You're going to stage a protest, or several protests? You probably need the special social skills of my cohorts and a seaworthy vessel like my Wilbur to pull it off?"

He gave me a crooked smile. "No, actually I want to blow the shit out of some things and I need a really crazy person to help me. I want you to take me inside and introduce me to Shark Hunter."

Chapter Eighteen

It took some explaining and convincing, but I finally decided to do it. Shawn told us he needed to talk to the man in the worst way. He'd heard Shark Hunter had a strong dislike for newspaper reporters and hoped I'd be able to do an intro since I was Hunter's biographer.

"Biographer?"

"Heard it from several people."

The final convincing came from Consuelo who was having a great time and said she wasn't leaving without a look inside. She'd never been in the Scorpion Pit, but her sisters had and told her about it. So we got in line at the front door.

Talking to the doorman were the bikers in charge of keeping an eye on all the parked motorcycles. Slip told me this duty was usually delegated to the one's who smelled too bad to let inside and those too insecure to be separated from their guns. A big sign by the door, "NO WEAPONS OR GUNS."

The doorman didn't want to let the yuppie-looking newspaperman inside until some credentials were shown in the form of a couple of twenties. Behind us in line teetered the two shaved heads who'd been trying to maim each other minutes before, now with arms around each other's shoulders, beer buddies.

Once inside I hesitated a second from the sensory assault of noise, smell, and sight. Something flew from my left to right a couple of feet in front of my eyes. Yells from the left and I saw the dart had found its mark, or close. A man against the opposite wall bent over displaying a big blue-jeaned ass with a red bull's-eye painted on. He reached back to pull out a thirty pointer as we walked by. We carefully stepped around broken chairs and prone bodies toward the stairs in back.

You could almost cut the testosterone in the air with a knife, something every other person in the bar seemed to have one of. Mostly your smaller, easy to conceal switchblades and stilettos. Some being used to pick nails or teeth, or else stuck in the bar within easy reach, still others being waved in someone's face.

An exceptionally good-looking woman in tight leather leaned against the bar surrounded by six alpha males in season, all holding drinks and giving everyone challenging looks. Half the people in the bar wearing black leather vests with no shirt underneath, women included.

The sprinkling of bar hags in attendance drew a good turnout from the abundant ranks of beta males. A few of the hags very likely trannies, at least one openly, she/he surrounded by a small group of badly tattooed men who looked like they'd been out of prison only a few hours.

We waited by the foot of the stairs while Slip got drinks. A blood-curdling scream came from the roof, then another.

"Y'all give me a hand here!"

We helped Slip with some pitchers of beer. No glasses or bottles upstairs at night, only plastic pitchers. The bartenders wearing bicycle helmets with fish clubs on their belts.

The roof area looked about the same as the last time I saw it, just darker with even more broken glass, but most of the tables upright and occupied.

At least it wasn't as noisy up top. Dark though, only a couple of bare bulbs for light. The loud music downstairs made the roof reverberate under our feet as we made our way across. I could see Shark Hunter holding court at his usual table with a few locals. Most of the bikers downstairs were trying hard to look repulsive; for the group sitting and slouching at the table, it came natural. One had his shirt off, sitting with his back to the old shark man, who looked up at me coming with a pitcher of beer.

"Taco Something!"

Everyone at the table looked. Shark Hunter held his hands out, wiggling fingers at my pitcher. "Mmmmm! Gimme!"

I sat the beer on the table in front of him and he immediately drank off almost half, belched, and went back to what he was doing.

Holding a small flashlight in the dim light, he would look over the man's body then use a smoking soldering iron with a glowing red tip to burn the man. The screams were pretty impressive. It took me a few seconds to figure out he was burning off small skin lesions.

The man put his shirt back on and handed over a twenty. Shark Hunter smiled and noticed me still standing there. Then he noticed Consuelo who had edged up for a closer look.

"How about you, little lady? Just take your shirt off for a free examination!"

Consuelo looked like she was thinking about it. Slip had wisely elected to stay in the shadows so the old man wouldn't see him. While everyone at the table eagerly waited for Consuelo to make up her mind, I pulled Shawn up close to the table.

"Mr. Hunter, this man here would like a word with you."

Shawn sat his full pitcher of beer on the table in front of the old man, who didn't take his eyes off Consuelo since she seemed about to decide.

"Well, I haven't been checked in a while."

Just as she pulled her shirt up, every man at the table turned on a small flashlight of his own. No bra. She turned completely around once before dropping the shirt back down. The flashlights all went off just as quickly.

"See any problems?"

Unanimous and hardy agreement from the table of doctoral candidates that everything looked mighty fine. They all took a long drink of beer. Shark made a mark on the low wall behind him then noticed Shawn for the first time.

"Where'd you come from?"

"Taco Bob brought me to meet you." A quick glance at me and a cautious nod.

"What you want?"

"I have something very important to talk to you about."

I got a bored look from the old man.

"Key West is in grave danger and you're the only one who can save it."

The old man pulled out a book and started reading with his flashlight. I had to jump in.

"Mr. Hunter, I think what the young man is trying to say is, he's looking for a charter."

That did it. The book snapped shut.

"Well, why didn't you say so! What kind of fishing you got in mind, partner?" Big smile for the prospective client.

"Uh, night fishing. Maybe even tonight."

Smile gone now, looking serious, "I'll need to check my schedule." The old charter captain stood up and walked a few steps, then sat down and held up a hand to count fingers. "I can walk and got five fingers, so I ain't too drunk and I ain't dreaming. I reckon we can give her a shot. Though my regular mate went overboard today, so I got no help."

I remembered the big man from my last visit.

"Baby fell overboard? Is he all right?"

"Not that kind of overboard, just went overboard on the jalapeno poppers at Gov's and came down with a bad case of the flaming trots. Last I seen, he was sitting in a bucket of ice."

Shawn picked up on it, saying the right things, "Not to worry, I've got several able-bodied people ready to help. Do you accept cash for your charters? Here's a down payment."

A c-note disappeared a split second after being offered.

"Cash is good. What kind of fish you after? Shark, I bet." Smiles and a wink.

Shawn had the ball now and was making a respectable run. He leaned in close. "No, not sharks. I'm after something much more dangerous." And let that hang.

The old man picked it up, "Ain't nothing more dangerous than sharks!"

Grumbled agreement from around the table. But Shawn was into it now, his voice rising.

"I'm looking to tear the heart out of a beast, a monstrous beast that has killed once and will kill again if it isn't stopped!" Fist hard on the table, spilling beer. "I need a good boat and a captain who isn't afraid to spit in the eye of the Devil himself and willing to take on the most dangerous monster that ever came to Key West!" Touchdown, six points.

No one at the table said anything, just looked nervous. The only sound the droning of music from below and thundering motorcycles in the parking lot. The man known as a killer of huge sharks glared at each man at the table with narrowed eyes.

"Blow!"

And they were gone.

He motioned for Shawn to sit. Maybe it was the light, but the young reporter looked older, his eyes a little crazy in the dim light. Still standing, he shook my hand.

"Thanks, Taco Bob. Mr. Hunter and I have to discuss some upcoming felonies, and I really don't want you or your friends to get any more involved in this than you already are. In fact, you might want to forget about this evening."

I didn't bother to tell him we might be having a personal audience with representatives of Blue Manatee later on. I figured he had enough to think about already with whatever he and Mr. Hunter might be about to get into. I wished him luck and headed out with Consuelo close behind.

Slip sat waiting over by the stairs, next to him a woman back in the shadows I hadn't noticed when we came in. The woman attractive in an anorexic, Goth way, nattering on to Slip while protecting a martini with long red fingernails and holding a cigarette stuck in a phallic-looking holder. Slip jumped up, anxious to go.

We followed Slip down the stairs, the place even nois-ier and more crowded. But we made it through the melee and almost to the door. That's where Slip spotted the two Blue Manatee goons just coming in. One had a big white X bandage over his broken nose and was hard to miss. Especially hard for Slip to miss.

As soon as he saw the guy, he ran over and started punching him in the face again. I tried to grab Consuelo, but she squirted out of my grasp and ran over and got in front of the other one to keep him off Slip. The guy spit in her face. The petite hotel proprietress brought a knee up into the guy's crotch so hard his feet came off the floor a bit. He bent over in agony enough for her to grab two handfuls of hair and give him another knee just as hard in the face. He staggered off and fell into the dart players.

By then Slip had Mr. X on the floor, doing some clog steps on his head, so the two of us grabbed the dancing fishing guide and dragged him out the door before one of the bouncers got there with a ball bat.

Heading for the car, I gave them each a look. Consuelo was wiping her face off on her shirt. I was not particularly happy.

"Well, that was close. I thought for a minute there we might actually get out of that place without you two starting a fight."

We walked by the two guys with shaved heads back at it again, whaling away at each other on the edge of the parking lot.

Slip just shrugged, "I figured with that big X on his face, someone would be taking a shot at him before long anyway."

He did have a point. That X was sure to draw a fist or a dart.

Consuelo was still flushed from the fight, strutting a little now as we got to the car. "New girlfriend you were talking to, Slip?"

"Yeah, right. I was just trying to stay away from that crazy shark guy. I'd been talking to the stick chick's boyfriend. He was in the shadows taking a crap over the wall when you stopped by on your way out."

I got the car unlocked and we piled in.

Slip wasn't done. "I was keeping an eye on things though, seen the newspaper guy got his meet. Also saw you showing your chest bumps to the dregs of society."

"Hey, I just wanted everyone to feel comfortable, you know, do my part."

Slip started to say something that would likely start an argument I didn't want to hear, so I held up my hand. I kicked the little car in the ass and we sped out of the parking lot.

"How about we talk about the rest of the evening's entertainment, as in the possibility of one of those previously mentioned Blue Manatee enforcement teams stopping by?"

Chapter Nineteen

By the time I was sure I was alone and hadn't had any visitors, I was worn out. Mary Ann was still on my mind and not in a good way. Coming back from the bar, I realized I'd forgotten to ask Shawn about the mention of JB in the note, and we still didn't know what happened to his sister.

I really needed to get some sleep, some sound sleep, but the night wasn't over. I left all the lights on inside my cozy houseboat while I made a phone call, some coffee, and a sandwich.

An hour later I turned out all the lights except the bathroom light. I gave that a few minutes, then turned it off and moved quietly up through the roof hatch onto the bridge. I set my supplies on the floor within easy reach and got comfortable lying where I had the best view of the dock. Everything quiet now, just the distant tapping of stainless lines on the masts of sailboats in the dim light.

Five minutes later the phone in my pocket vibrated and I looked at my watch. Somehow over two hours had slipped by. I looked along the dock and saw two men walk straight to my houseboat and carefully step aboard. I was coming awake fast and trying to wait until I could see the whites of their eyes. A second later I hit the switch on the one million candlepower spotlight and got the first one right in the face. His partner a step behind held up his hand but he got some of it too. I was so nervous I didn't do the yelled voice quite right, but it still did the trick.

"Wake up, Johnny! There they are! Shoot 'em! Give 'em both barrels!"

The blinded one fell trying to get off the boat and cracked his head on the dock. He came up holding his head with one hand and a gun in the other. Both had guns out now, running. I killed the light and watched them run out of the marina into the gloom. Two figures in the dark following a safe distance behind.

I heard an engine start and a short peel of rubber. I went below and flipped on some lights and set a few things on the coffee table in front of the yellow couch. A minute later the boat moved and my two wild-eyed cohorts burst into the lounge. I pointed toward the low table. Consuelo grabbed the pencil and pad I'd set out and scribbled furiously, then showed it to Slip who studied it for a second or two before nodding his approval. Then they both grabbed the cold beers waiting on the table and took long pulls.

"What were they driving?"

Consuelo wiped her mouth with the back of her hand and picked up the pad.

"Ford Mustang, dark blue or black, probably a rental. Got the tag, though." A sly smile as she handed me the pad. When I looked up from the pad, the smile was gone.

"They had guns." Slip holding his beer didn't look too happy either.

"They pulled guns when I put the light on 'em. I don't think they had 'em out when they came on board."

Slow nods.

"Want to hear the big news?" Consuelo holding a hand out, inspecting her nails. "Like, where they came from?"

Slip must have fallen asleep as well, which would explain the looks we were both getting.

She waited until we both nodded. "I didn't see them come from the direction of their car. They must have already been set up, waiting when we got back from the bar." A quick glance at her audience. "I hit the speed dial for your cell when I saw two men step off the boat three slips down and start walking this way."

Slip said it before I could get it out, "The asshole lawyer's boat?"

It took a while for us to wind down and get to bed. My partners wanted to go right then and roust Grizzel, but I was able to convince them to sleep on it. I'd decided to wait until the next day to tell them about my call earlier to Tony the Crab.

I'd already been thinking about making the call, and the young newspaperman saying something about there being more to DDT made the decision for me.

The number was for a seafood restaurant. I'd called late, but I could hear in the background that they were still busy. I asked if it was too late for a delivery of Crab Surprise. Asked just like I'd been instructed while standing in the sand spurs along U.S.1 one evening. There was a long pause on the other end, then I was told they'd call me back in a few minutes. I gave them my cell number and ten minutes later it rang.

"Taco, baby! How you doing?"

"Fine, Tony. I trust you're feeling better? You looked like you might be coming down with something the last time I saw you."

"Yeah, coming down off a bridge with a cinder block wired to my ankles plays hell with my allergies. But lucky for me the morons didn't know it was only five feet deep under that bridge. But hey, I'm doing better since my stay in the hospital. A few more visits with the plastic surgeon, I'll be good as new, maybe better."

"That's great, Tony. I was wondering if I could ask you a favor?"

"Please do, kid! I never forget when someone saves my life. I owe you big. Whatever you want, just name it."

"What I need is information. There's an outfit down here called Blue Manatee. They're barging in fill to build a big development adjoining Key West, building their own island, actually." I hadn't thought of it like that until then. "I think it's an outfit called DDT behind it. I need to know who's running DDT and anything I can find out about them."

"I don't understand. You want to apply for a job? What do you want with those people? Me, I'd strongly advise staying the fuck away from DDT."

"I have a high regard for your advice and would like to do just that, but they've been sending large, ugly men to watch my home lately, and I think things may be taking a turn for the worse soon. I'm not sure what I'm asking here, Tony. I guess knowing some names and where-abouts of the people behind DDT would be a help."

"Kid, all I know right off is these are some bad hom-bres, but I'll see what I can do. Let me make a couple calls and get back with you."

"Thanks, Tony."

"While you're waiting, you want I should have some-body whacked for you? Ex-wife? Boss? The President?"

"No, I don't want to put you out, Tony."

"Hey, no problemo! Glad to do it. How about a stock tip? Or a horse? Got one in the fifth at Gulfstream I'd bet my grandmother on."

"No, really ..."

"What about Hoffa? Want to know what he's up to these days? Or how about those inventions you hear about only once? You know, like some guy builds a car that runs off dog farts and sand, and then you never hear about him again? Want to know what happens to those people? I got the inside dope on lots of interesting shit, all you have to do is ask."

"I'll keep it in mind."

The call came around three am. I'd taken the cell-phone into the bedroom with me after the excitement ear-lier with the two armed men. I was having another night-mare when it rang. I hoped it didn't wake anyone else. Tony sounded different.

"I had to call in a couple of big favors here and found out some shit I wish I didn't know. These DDT whack-offs are just a front. This development you mentioned? It's just for starters. The big picture has Key West as you know it swallowed up completely pretty quick. Sanitized is the word my sources used, and not in a good way." He went quiet for a few beats.

"The master plan has them filling most of the shallow water all the way to the Dry Tortugas. These people are talking a new six-lane highway through the Keys, a major jet-port in Key West, and cruise ships by the hundreds. It seems being the only Caribbean island hooked up to the U.S. mainland has tremendous potential."

I could hear him breathing hard on the other end of the line.

"Look, kid, you said you live on a houseboat? I'd strongly advise you pull anchor and get the fuck out of Dodge real soon. These are some very scary people. In fact, I may have to lay low for a while myself now that I stuck my nose in it. My sources said these people really got their shorts in a bunch about someone writing a book about someone they whacked. I'd hate to be that guy, if you know what I mean. Take care of yourself, kid." He was about to hang up.

"Wait, Tony, you didn't tell me who's behind all this."

There was just static, I was afraid he'd hung up.

"Okay. After this we're even, got it? I don't even want to say the name of this bunch of assholes, but that six-lane highway? It comes from Orlando."

"You mean?"

"Yep, they're going to turn Key West into a giant theme park."

Chapter Twenty

The next morning I woke up groggy from another bad nightmare when someone kept beating on the bedroom door. It felt like buzzards had been roosting in my mouth, and I could barely get out of bed to let Slip in. He gave me the eye.

"Oh, shit, partner. You ain't looking too hot."

Actually, I was hot, burning up. I managed to make it back to the bed. Consuelo came in and felt my forehead.

"Well, he's got a fever and looks like death eating a cracker. I say he's sick."

Slip nodded in agreement.

"You better stay in bed. Slip, see if you can find a thermometer in the first-aid kit."

I didn't have a real firm grasp on the passage of time or what was going on right then. Later on it was determined by Consuelo's sister, who actually knew about such things, that I'd had a relapse of swamp fever brought on by lack of sleep and stress. Bed rest, antibiotics, and plenty of fluids were prescribed.

As the day went on I only felt worse. I was so weak I had to have help getting to the bathroom. I knew there were things that required my immediate attention, but I was almost helpless and kept slipping in and out of nightmares. My mind was a blur of concerns about Mary Ann and what was happening to Key West. At one point it suddenly came to me what had been causing my nightmares but I couldn't hold onto the thought, it kept slipping away to play with the zombies, manatees, teamsters, voodoo dolls, and murderous cartoon characters dancing through my fevered brain.

At one point I smelled something nice, something familiar. I gathered all my energy and opened one eye enough to see Consuelo lying next to me on the bed. Little sobs coming as she lightly rubbed the same place on my shoulder over and over. Another time I saw Slip sitting next to the bed reading a book.

I woke again later and found myself alone in the room. I slipped down to the floor. Too weak to stand, I crawled to the corner farthest from the bed and fell right back to sleep. I woke from a terrible nightmare in bed with my fishing partners in the room watching me. Both looked really worried, especially Slip.

"How you doing, ol' fella? We found you on the floor."

"I know. The bed makes me sick." My voice weak, just a whisper. They exchanged looks. Consuelo sat on the bed.

"Taco, you need to stay in bed so you'll get better."

"No. Get me to the couch." Arguing with either of these two was bad enough when I was well, I didn't have the strength to spare. "I had a dream. I'll die if I stay in this bed." I didn't really have that dream, but I did know I had to get away from the bed.

They finally relented, and I slept hard on the couch for several hours. When I came to, it was dark outside and the jackhammer headache had come down a couple of notches. I could open my eyes without thinking my head was about to split open. Consuelo walked by and saw I was awake.

"Hey. You feeling better?" She sat down next to me on the sofa and put her hand on my forehead. "Still hot. You've been delirious. As soon as Slip gets back, we'll help you back to bed."

It took all of my strength, but I moved her cool hand back to my forehead and held it there. "No, right here is fine. No bed." Her hand felt so good, I'm sure I smiled before going back to sleep.

I came to again later and realized the cool hand was now a washcloth. The pain in my head had eased a bit more. I tried to sit up and the pain came right back. Consuelo appeared and handed me a couple of aspirin and a cup of water. She helped me sit, and I finally got the aspirin down.

"Any better?"

"A little. As long as I don't move."

She helped me lay back down. I felt like a helpless baby in her strong arms. Things were coming to me that I always seemed too busy to notice before. "You're strong." I smiled. "You're also very beautiful, Consuelo. I guess I never really —"

The door opened and Slip barged in. Consuelo, the beautiful goddess holding my hand, looked at him. I couldn't see the look aimed at poor Slip, but I felt her body tense when the door opened, and Slip went backwards about a foot like he'd been punched in the chest.

"Oops! Hope I'm not interrupting." Slip looked really nervous, like he might need to borrow the fire extinguisher again. "Taco, something's going on down the dock by the Wilbur, and there's a cop out here needs to see you."

I didn't feel up to another visit from the cops. Probably got a report I was hiding nuclear bombs in my bathroom. Consuelo took it.

"Slip, for crying out loud, tell the man TB's sick and for him to come back later."

"Okay." Slip closed the door behind him but was back a minute later, looking worried. "Y'all ain't gonna like this. He says there's been a murder, another Marty. Says they found the body on the Wilbur, and he's here to arrest Taco."

I was in no condition to go anywhere, so getting hauled down to the police station didn't do me a lot of good. My bad luck held as the same cop who had seen me looking for Julie at her dead brother's house was the arresting officer. I guess he thought I was faking sick.

I managed to stay conscious through the interrogation, but the pain in my head got so bad I eventually dry heaved and passed out.

There was a light in my eyes. A spotlight passed over me, then over the rest of the crowd seated in the big ballroom. A booming voice filled the room.

"And now the moment you've all been waiting for: The John D. MacDonald Award for Best Florida Novel Ever Written! Presenting the award, last year's winner, Carl Hiaasen!"

Everyone was clapping like crazy. Mr. Hiaasen stood there smiling while the applause went on and on. I was at a table in front and had to look up. The man must have been at least ten feet tall.

When the crowd finally settled down and let him get in a word, he started in about how honored he was to present the award, how important the award was, and then just as he made for the home stretch of getting to the point, he looked right at me and I knew I'd won. That's when I noticed I didn't have on any pants.

The applause started again after Mr. Hiaasen said my name. He pointed at me and motioned for me to join him on stage. I didn't have on any underwear either.

Just as the panic was making it hard for me to breathe, I passed out.

My feet were wet and my head hurt. I was outside, on an old dock with my bare feet dangling in the warm water.

"You don't need all that crap! All that fame just makes a man take himself far too seriously anyway."

I looked around to see who was talking. A big, good-looking guy holding a fishing pole sat a few feet down the dock. Man looked like he'd seen his share and then some of tough scrapes.

"That fame can make you lose sight of the important things in life. You're better off the way you are, believe me." He reeled in a sizable trout, then tossed it back in the water.

"Shoot, most people work so hard for so long, they finally get retired, they don't know what to do with themselves." He reeled in a six-foot sailfish, looked it over, tossed it back.

"Poor bastards spend most of their time trying to convince themselves they enjoy golf, or else just sit around bored to tears. Half the time they go back to work just so they'll have something to do." Another cast and another fish. This time a black marlin the size of a Buick. He showed me the fish and gave me a thumbs up before dropping it back in the water.

"You take my advice and grab some time off whenever you can. Take your retirement in installments while you're still young enough to enjoy the booze, the fishing, and especially the women." He gave me a big wink and started saying something about the clothes locker on my houseboat but stopped.

The guy looked dead at me with slate gray eyes. "That big yacht with the twins, the one that came in a few days ago. That's the ticket." Just then something big grabbed his line and pulled him off the dock and under the water. I noticed I was naked again.

Something nipped at my toe, then all my toes. I couldn't get my feet out of the water, they were stuck. I looked down and there were dozens of little blue manatees wearing mouse ears, and they were eating my feet. Up to this point I'd thought manatees were gray, bigger, and vegetarians.

About the time I finally had the sense to look at my hands and count fingers to see if I was dreaming, I came to, in the hospital. The door woke me.

"How you feeling?"

"Like a doormat at a cattle stampede. How long I been out?"

"Couple days. Consuelo's working a shift at the hotel, she should be getting off soon though. She's pretty upset with the police." Slip didn't look too happy with them either, and I already knew how I felt. "Doc here at the hospital said you were talking in your sleep earlier when he shined a light in your eyes."

"What did I say?"

"Something about your pants."

"Am I still under arrest?"

"I'm afraid so." Slip started picking through an untouched food tray by the bed. "The Marty Manatee, the one who came up with that song about Blue Manatee they been playing on the radio? He's the one they found dead on the deck of the Wilbur. Blunt instrument to the head. Your heavy flashlight was lying next to the body."

"I remember some of that from my visit to the police station." It took me a minute to put it together. "The flashlight. That time we came back and I said someone had been on the houseboat?"

"Exactly. Pretty classic frame-up, I'd say."

"And they think I did it?"

"Looks like their extensive investigation has it narrowed down to you, and not much else. But I heard the time of death and some other crime scene stuff puts the man murdered with your flashlight somewhere else, then dumped on board the Wilbur."

"The two who tried to come on my houseboat?"

"Could be. They might've been pissed enough about getting scared off like that to come back and get sloppy. We seen to it the cops got some anonymous tips on the car those two were driving, but they're mighty hard-headed, still thinking you done it." Slip sniffed a piece of bacon from the tray, then ate it. "They been getting real interested in Blondie and me lately. I think they're want-ing to try to pin JB on the three of us. We been advised not to leave town." He selected some toast and made what looked like a grits sandwich. "This ain't bad for hospital food."

The door opened — Consuelo.

"Hey, you're awake! How do —" She saw the food tray and Slip poking the sandwich in his mouth as fast as he could. "Slip! You're eating Taco's food? The man is on death's door and you're eating his food?"

She had him by the ear, twisting, which wasn't helping him swallow. I tried not to laugh since I knew it would hurt. My voice was still weak, "Consuelo."

She turned loose of Slip and an instant later was perched on the edge of the bed, holding my hand in hers. I gave it a little squeeze.

"I need to talk to you both. That yacht, the one that pulled in next to the Wilbur a few days ago? The police talked to those people, didn't they?" Slip sat in a chair by the bed while keeping a wary eye on my hand holder. Consuelo shook her head.

"The one with the twins? It's gone, but you're right, I think it was there that night. They must have left the next day, before the cops found the body."

She looked at Slip, then me.

"You think they had something to do with the murder?"

I was still trying to remember the crazy dream. "No, but remember the father?"

Slip grunted. "Yeah, never seen a man more protective of his daughters. Them two teenage girls looked like trouble on the hoof, ready to jump ship the first time the old man turned his back. No wonder he had that fancy boat of his set up with all those alarms and surveillance cameras and stuff."

Consuelo picked it up before I could. "Of course! With the way he kept that boat lit up at night, chances are one of those cameras caught anything going on aboard the Wilbur." She pulled out her cell and started pushing numbers. "What was the name of that boat?"

Slip smiled big. "*Eye Candy Too* as I well remember. Out of Miami. Shouldn't be hard to find."

The cop that'd been outside in the hall came in and said visiting time was over; my companions would have to leave. This got him some hard looks, but they headed out a few minutes later, Consuelo still on the phone with a Detective Gonzales.

The door woke me again a few hours later. Slip came in, acting sneaky. "How about a beer?" He pulled a long-neck from under his shirt, wiped it off and opened it. Then took one out for himself. I tried a sip, it was damn good.

"How'd you get this past the hospital people, not to mention the cop?"

Even bigger smile. "No cop! I'm proud to say you're once again a free man. The owner of the yacht came through with the video. May I be struck down if I ever say anything bad about overprotective fathers again!"

"All clear then?"

"Yep, videotape had two big fellas hauling the dead guy on the Wilbur and putting the flashlight down on the deck. Before hauling ass they looked around and right at the camera. Cops had to admit it wasn't you, me, or Consuelo." Slip looked happy as a clam, and rightly so.

There wasn't much doubt in my mind the ones who did it worked for Blue Manatee. "I would imagine those two are laying low, maybe out of town by now."

"Well, that'll give the cops something to do. Consuelo's back at the hotel, but you got another visitor."

He got up and stuck his head out the door for a second. Everything was still a bit slow for me, so when I looked up there was Jimmy Redd. He was smiling as usual, but the smile was different.

"How you doing, Taco? Heard you got a touch of the fever." Jimmy took the chair close to the bed.

"I been better. Luckily I got some excellent care."

Slip spoke up. "Speaking of, Doc says your fever is down and you might be able to go home this evening."

It was good to hear someone thought I might be doing better, since I sure didn't feel much better. I had to talk slow. "That's good. I reckon I'll be on my feet again in a few days."

Jimmy had the nervous thing going again. "If you feel up to it, I need to talk to you about something, in private."

This sounded a little unusual, but after assurances he'd be just outside if I needed something, Slip left Jimmy and me alone.

"TB, I need your help."

"You got it, Jimmy. So long as you aren't needing a partner for racketball this afternoon."

He gave up a small smile. Something was up.

"A few days ago Slip said someone had been on your boat, looking for something."

Makes sense Slip would tell Jimmy to keep an eye out. I nodded but didn't say anything.

"Then there's a body on your fishing boat. Your flashlight the murder weapon."

"Yeah, we put that together. Someone going to a lot of trouble to get me arrested."

He got up and paced some, peeked out the window. He looked like a man with a lot on his mind. When he'd said he wanted to talk, I figured women problems, that or he had a mostly legal business proposition. I was wrong.

"Taco, how much do you know about Blue Manatee?"

"Not a whole lot, some. Looks like they're going to bring some big changes to this town and I reckon some folks aren't too happy about it."

"Yeah, big changes."

He sat there looking at his hands for a minute. I didn't mind the break, I had another wave of fever nausea to deal with right then anyway.

"There's more going on here than people know."

He appeared to be having trouble getting something out, so I tried to keep things moving. "You said you needed my help."

He looked up and seemed to come to a decision. "Yeah, I do. You see, Blue Manatee is actually run by an outfit called DDT." I didn't want to be rude, but my fevered mind craved rest and another visit from the blond care-giver I had only recently acquired a better appreciation for.

"Jimmy, I kinda know a lot of that already, maybe more than I'd like to know, in fact." We locked eyes. "I know who's behind DDT."

This got his attention, especially when I put my hands on my head to make mouse ears. He smiled his first real smile.

"Ah, great! Well, then, you might know that in addition to being a laid-back lounge singer who's popular with the ladies and lives on a sailboat, I'm also a federal agent." He handed over an ID card with a star on it.

"Uh, no. Can't say I knew that right off. Nice ID, looks real." My feverish brain was having trouble with this.

"Oh, it's real. Remember how I went to California for that record deal?"

"You got signed and the record guy got arrested?"

"Yeah, but he was in jail before I got the money. I didn't get a dime." He shrugged. "One of the feds on that case knew someone who was hiring for the NSA. Since I didn't even have money to get back to Key West, I went to the interview and, after a few weeks of training, came back here. I've been on Uncle Sam's nickel since."

"That might explain why a boat bum has such a nice wardrobe."

He lit up a big smile this time. "I wondered if you might be curious about that."

"A little. What does NSA stand for? You some kind of spy?"

"In my case it stands for No Such Agency. Of course you can't let this leave the room."

The serious looks were back. I pointed toward the door where my friend had gone.

"No, not even them. We'll just say I had a shaky business proposition for you."

"Which might be the truth, since you never did tell me what kind of help you need."

"A couple of things, actually. One — I need to get on Grizzel's boat. I know there's a rivalry between you two about your book." I started to protest, but he continued, "If you can just get him and anyone else off that boat for an hour or two, that should do it. His specialty has always been illegal phone taps. If we can get hold of any recordings of his phone conversations, I'm hoping we can nail

Blue Manatee for kidnapping, murder, and the big one —
tax evasion. I'm pretty sure he's up to his neck with the
people behind Blue Manatee. If we can get something on
him, he'll probably rat them out to save his own skin. A
lawyer testifying against these people wouldn't be safe in
prison. He's smart enough to know the witness protection
program is his only hope."

"So you don't think he'll be prosecuted, even if he's
implicated in murder?"

"Probably not. The way these things work, if he rolls
over he'll likely end up in some place like Dayton, Ohio,
selling insurance or used cars." Jimmy gave me a look
like, What can you do?

"You said two things?" Not that my impaired brain
needed more to work on.

"There's some people here in Key West, like you said,
who aren't too happy about Blue Manatee. This being Key
West, they're likely to file a complaint in a very direct
manner." Another look in the eyes. "You need to call off
Shark Hunter and his gang, at least until I see what's on
Grizzel's houseboat. If they do anything before that, these
people will likely go to ground and I may never get
another chance."

"Shark Hunter and his gang?"

"It's my job to know what everyone in Key West is up
to."

I realized he was in a good position to do just that.

"You put Clarence Hunter and the newspaperman
together, didn't you?"

I nodded.

"Word on the street has them hanging out a lot the
last couple of days, having secret meetings with people

around town, and going out on that old boat at night. I'm sure they're up to something, something big."

"Well, I wouldn't be too surprised. I think between 'em they got enough initiative and crazy to do about anything." I still hadn't quite got a handle on all this. "Why do you need help from me? Don't you have some Seal teams or FBI agents for this sort of thing?"

"Not really. Budget cutbacks, you know. In fact, I'm having a hard time convincing my bosses to move on the case. Not enough dead bodies for action on such a big outfit. I think they have a body-to-corporate-earnings ratio they use to determine these things. That and they have to meet with lobbyists to figure in past and projected political campaign contributions. It's all pretty complicated, and slow." Another shrug. "However, the IRS would be very interested if I can prove that one of their most wanted is back."

"The IRS has a most wanted list?"

"Yeah. I think they're coming out with a TV show in the fall." He didn't look like he was kidding. "Remember Uncle Walt? One of their biggest cases. He owed millions when he died."

"Seems like he was cryogenically frozen, or something."

"Yeah, he was. Uncle Walt was a pioneer in several fields besides cartoon animation and theme parks. He also broke new ground in tax evasion. He was the first to have himself declared legally dead so he could skip out on paying income tax."

"You're shitting me."

"Nope. I've been hearing for a while now he's back — unfrozen. Word is he wants to move his main operation as far south as he can and still be in the US. I guess even though the man is trying to beat his country out of all those back taxes, he's still patriotic deep inside." Jimmy smiled, "And I would imagine after what must have felt like a forty-year-long ice-cold shower, he's ready for some tropical sunshine and warm breezes."

Chapter Twenty-One

Jimmy told me more about Uncle Walt, DDT, Blue Manatee, and their long-range plans for Key West. I told him about the dreamer and the environmentalists. He just shrugged.

"These people have so many resources and such an extensive operation, it's not surprising that they would infiltrate the tree huggers as well as the local politicians. They've probably also gotten to some people in law enforcement, on all levels, which is another reason I need your help. I know you're not on their payroll, or they wouldn't be killing people to set you up."

"Yeah, there's that. Nothing like getting set up for a murder rap to make a man feel law-abiding."

We started kicking around some ideas for getting Grizzel and whatever Blue Manatee people off that houseboat as soon as possible. It took all my energy to get it thought out.

"Let me rest up a bit, and I'll see if I can get my cohorts to help without spilling any beans about your employment. They're neither one too fond of Grizzel, and I'm sure they'd jump at any chance to inconvenience the man."

"Maybe you can get him in some kind of contest. He sees himself as the world's greatest sportsman, not to mention he thinks he's God's gift to women."

"Yeah, I'll try to come up with something along those lines. Maybe kill a couple of birds here. Sounds like I got to see Mr. Hunter anyway."

"Good. Let me know what you come up with tomorrow morning? I have a few things you can borrow if you need to. Some experimental stuff for the military."

I was asleep before he got out the door.

"So let me get this straight. Consuelo here is going to convince Grizzel to go with you, and you want me to help Jimmy take Grizzel's computer and files as a kind of joke on the man?" Slip gave this some hard thought. "Do we get to sink his boat too?"

"No."

"Set it on fire?"

I shook my head.

"Just a small fire?"

"No, nothing like that. Jimmy just thought it would be a fun way to get back at Grizzel for being such an asshole."

"Seems a little too easy for any real fun."

"Well, as we've seen, these days there seems to be some traffic over there of the Blue Manatee variety. Might be someone there guarding the place when Grizzel leaves."

This seemed to make Slip a little happier. I was happy myself just to be back home.

"Okay. Maybe I can take a quick look at the engines on that thing while we're there. I've heard it run, sounds like twin diesels."

"We'll see how it goes. Do some thinking on how you're going to get on board if there's a guard."

A well-practiced sloppy salute and the man was out on the aft deck for some hard planning. Consuelo had been rustling around in the kitchen trying to keep up with whatever she was doing and with what we were saying. She came and sat by the couch with a steaming cup of something.

"Try this. I got the recipe from Sara. Supposed to be a really good soup for sick people." After a good night's sleep on the couch, I was still mighty weak but definitely feeling better.

"It's good. I think I might have had this before." I smiled and was handed a stack of mail. On the top was a letter from Mary Ann. A small square, embossed envelope.

"Aren't you going to open it?"

"Maybe later. You and I need talk about how we can get Grizzel off that houseboat for a couple of hours."

It didn't take long. Along with her other attributes, it seems Consuelo can also be quite devious. She blames it on her sisters.

After we had our plan hammered out, I called Jimmy; he told me to hold tight, he'd be right over. I sent my two associates on a grocery and supply run just before Jimmy came by. Less than twenty minutes later, everything was worked out and I was alone with the mail, the unopened letter from Mary Ann still on the top.

"I called Mary Ann and left a message when you first took sick. What was in the letter?" Slip and I were waiting on Consuelo to get back. I couldn't see much of Grizzel's boat from the lounge window, but I took a look every few minutes anyway.

"Wedding invitation."

"Huh? For — "

"Her and some guy from work."

"Oh shit, partner. I'm sorry to hear that."

"Don't tell Consuelo, okay?"

"Okay. That sure does suck."

I agreed.

The soup did make me feel better. In fact, other than I still only had the strength of a two-year-old and felt like my heart had been ripped out with a pair of pliers, I was fine. Or at least a bit more clear-headed.

I took another glance out the window. If my cell phone so much as peeped, the cavalry, in the form of one Slip Hanson, would be out the door at a run. But it stayed silent, and after a while I saw Consuelo coming back down the dock flashing a smile and giving me a covert thumb's up.

"Looks like our gal did it. I just need to go see Shark Hunter and get things set up on that end. You might want to wait here, since you and him ..."

"No problem. I need to take a look in the clothes locker anyway, see what I can come up with for my disguise."

Consuelo parked where I showed her outside the gate of the abandoned marina. After a short and heated debate, she agreed to wait in the car. Not that I really thought it would be any safer. I just didn't want her to get any more involved in the mess than absolutely necessary.

"Here, Consuelo, take this."

I handed over a small silver weapon that looked something like a pistol.

"What is this thing?" She didn't seem to be overly impressed.

"It's a kind of laser stun gun thing. Works like a regular stun gun up to ten feet away." She gave it a hard look and made a little snort laugh.

"This shouldn't take too long. Cell phone set?"

We both checked.

"Good. Don't use that unless you have to. It's experimental and not available to the general public. You can only get those from the military special forces and biker swap meets."

She lost the smile and her eyes softened.

"Be careful."

Before I knew it she'd leaned over and planted a real nice kiss on me. It was such a surprise, it took me a second to realize what was going on. A large percentage of my still weak body wanted to stay right there in the strong arms of the soft young woman, but I managed somehow to get out of the car and head for the gate.

The trail through the tall weeds and abandoned hulks looked like it had seen some use recently. I could see a couple of cars parked behind a crumbling tin building, and once I thought I saw movement on top of a derelict trawler.

When I got to the narrow board plank going out to Shark Hunter's boat, the man himself stood on deck waiting for me.

"Come on aboard! Wondering when you'd be coming to join us!"

I carefully negotiated the plank and took the offered hand for a rousing shake. The old shark fisherman looked over his shoulder toward the cabin door.

"See here, I told you Taco Something would be coming by!"

He turned loose of my hand, then grabbed an arm and about dragged me inside the cabin. Shawn the newspaperman looked up from a table full of charts long enough for a quick nod. On the floor was Queequeg giving me a welcoming growl. And sitting cross-legged on one of the bunks up front was Julie, cleaning what appeared to be an assault rifle. She sprang to her feet and went for the clinch, about to hug the stuffing out of me.

"Taco Bob! I'm so glad to see you!"

Finally I was in a position to find out exactly what had happened to her. But before I could ask, Julie took a step back and held my hands. I was again able to breathe.

"Those bastards Blue Manatee kidnapped me! Kept me all alone in a small room with only a toilet, a mini bar, and no cable for two days! It was terrible!" She blushed a little. "You know, the only thing that kept me going was thinking about how nice you'd been to me that night I came by your houseboat."

She had a new look going. Kind of a Rambo meets Victoria Secret that was quite fetching. She smelled of perfume and gun oil.

"I finally escaped by using the toilet tank lid on one of the guards. But I didn't know where to go. I was afraid of the police so I started walking toward the marina to see you again. One of my exes saw me and gave me a ride with him. I've been here since."

I had to ask, "One of your exes?"

She pointed with her thumb over her shoulder at Shawn, who gave a little wave without looking up from his calculations.

"He said he gave you a note, in the park? Told you I was okay and not to worry."

I got it then. Same first initial, same last name as her brother.

Shark Hunter stood out on the deck mumbling. I noticed he had a headset on, talking low to someone. He looked over at me.

"That gal you left in the car, that the same lil blond with you in the bar the other night?"

I nodded, "I was hoping to have a word with you, Mr. Hunter, just the two of us."

Julie was still standing in front of me gazing into my eyes in a dreamy way. She said, "We can talk later," and gave me a wet one square on the lips before going back to cleaning her gun.

The after-effects of the fever along with catching a good whiff of Queequeg, not to mention the sudden upturn in the amount of personal attention from attractive young women, had me feeling a bit dizzy. I went out into the cockpit with the old shark man and had a seat on the stern.

"You feeling okay, Taco?"

"I'm fine, Mr. Hunter. I had a bit of swamp fever come back on me a few days ago is all."

"Since you're joining up with us, there ain't no sense in being all formal. You can just call me Shark."

"Well, Shark, I was wanting to see about a charter more than actually joining up with your gang."

"I'm kinda booked already. I'm giving Shawn a special rate the next few days since he's part of the gang and all. You join up, there're lots of bennies."

He started winking and motioning with his head toward Julie while giving me the universal hand sign for the old in-and-out.

"Shawn says she tends to get infatuated kinda easily, but she does seem mighty sweet on you."

I looked in the cabin and saw Julie smiling at me while stuffing bullets in a banana clip. I got back to business.

"You know that lawyer, Harry Grizzel, lives on a fancy houseboat over at the marina?"

"I heard a one like that what's a grade-A asswipe."

"That's him. I need a half-day charter tomorrow morning. Kind of a fishing contest between him and me."

"Well, shit. Normally I'd jump at something like that, but we kinda got plans already. Real secret stuff, you know. Of course, if you was to join the gang I reckon I could tell you."

"I need to talk to you about that too. There's some other things in the works. Things that might put a halt to all that development and send some Blue Manatee folks to jail for JB's murder. They're worried you go to messing around, you might scare the bad guys enough they'd start getting a little too careful."

This got me another round of the steady eye and roving eye treatment.

"We do aim to have a lil surprise party for some folks, but I kinda doubt we're much open for any changes in our itinerary at this point. Plans is plans and all, you know."

"I got you. However, I think if you could work in this charter in the morning, the folks I've been talking to wouldn't try to get in the way if you had some plans for tomorrow night."

"Well, I reckon I need to call a meeting then, since I suppose you need to know something right away."

I gave a nod.

"I gotta call in the lookout. You interested in maybe being an honorary member of the gang long enough to stand watch while me and the rest have our meet?"

"Sure. In fact, I could probably talk Consuelo into doing it instead, in case y'all have any questions for me."

"The lil blond gal? Hell yeah! I done seen her credentials," I got a big wink. "I reckon I could just make you both honorary members for a couple hours."

I sat out in the cockpit while the lot of them had a closed-door meeting in the cabin. The lookout Consuelo relieved for the meeting turned out to be Danny the Dreamer, still a little spaced but smiling a lot. After just a few minutes I heard the old man yelling at me.

"Taco! Come on in here!" I went inside and left the door open, hoping Queequeg would take a walk. He didn't, so I stayed close to the door and breathable air. Shawn had put the charts away, his face a storm of suspicion.

"Who's this that wants us to play nice and take a scummy lawyer fishing? We had some plans for tonight. Big plans."

This got some grunts and snickers from the assembled group.

"Shawn, I can appreciate your concern, but I'm gonna have to say I can't say."

This wasn't too well received.

"But it's someone I trust who's representing them."

Shawn pulled at his goatee while pondering this. He needed more.

"Can you give us a hint?"

"Okay. Let's just say it's the same outfit that brings the mail."

"The post office?"

"The feds."

Immediately everyone in the room had a weapon out and looked ready to use it. The dog had a teeth-showing growl going.

"Hold the phone, folks! I think it's mostly the IRS, and they aren't interested in you anyway."

There was a distinct air of disappointment in the room. Guns, knives and at least one machine gun slipped back out of view.

"You let Shark do this charter tomorrow, and I think they might be willing to look the other way at anything y'all might have cooked up for Blue Manatee."

They didn't look too convinced, so I threw in a little joke. "I mean, as long as you're not going to blow up Key West or anything."

Which was met with blank stares all around.

An hour later we left the old marina with things set, or mostly set. I needed to get Consuelo up to speed on a

few things while she drove us over to take a look at what
Blue Manatee was up to.

"I think we got things worked out. The old shark man
is taking me and Grizzel out in the morning. That should
give Slip and Jimmy plenty of time to do what they're
going to do."

"I'm coming with you tomorrow."

It wasn't a question, and I didn't really have a good
reason why she shouldn't come along. I didn't want to
say, but as lousy as I still felt, it might not be a bad idea to
have her around.

"Okay. His mate is in the hospital, so it's probably just
Shark, us, and Grizzel."

"Sounds like a fun trip." She looked away from the
road to give me a sick look. "How many are in Shark's
outfit anyway?"

"You seen Danny when you took the lookout post, and
like I told you, Julie's with them. And of course Shawn
the newspaper guy, who's actually the brains of the operation. Levita's part of it somehow. Shark told me before I
left that she's been in a deep trance for two days, laying as
much bad ju-ju on Blue Manatee as she can."

We did a drive-by on the Blue Manatee park. I was surprised there wasn't more done on the fill island since I'd
seen it last. The short stretch of causeway was finished, but
the actual area of fill wasn't all that big. We swung around
and got a look from a different angle and could see dozens
of the huge sand barges lined up out on the horizon. Consuelo answered my question before I could ask.

"Had a bad storm with some wind while you were
out. Slowed things down a little. Maybe Levita conjured
up the storm."

I thought that was kind of funny, but the lady behind the wheel looked dead serious. Maybe I was just tired.

"I think I'll have a little lay-down when we get back to the marina. Maybe this evening we'll go over Slip and Jimmy's bit and you can stop by Grizzel's to remind him."

"It really pisses me off Blue Manatee, or DDT, or whoever, is getting away with all this." Her jaw was set and I got a shot of the fierce look in her eyes. "We've got to make this work."

I was too tired to give that any thought, much less a response.

Chapter Twenty-Two

I woke up on the couch. Consuelo was banging pots in the galley, and Slip was across the room watching the news on TV. I saw a blond head peek around the galley doorway, then more clanging before she came and sat next to me on the couch. I must have been out a while, since it was getting dark outside.

"How do you feel?" A cool hand on my forehead.

"Good, just weak still."

"I've got just the thing!"

She bounced back into the galley and I noticed her shorts. Kind of shorts wanting to be a thong. Slip turned off the television and came over and took a chair.

"We didn't want to wake you and I didn't want her going over there after dark. The shorts were her idea. She said they worked on Grizzel."

A big smile over a steaming cup of soup came my way from the galley.

"Yeah, Grizzel Dear did seem a little preoccupied with my apparel while I was reminding him about his chance tomorrow to show me what a big strong fisherman he is."

I shook my head.

"You were wearing that old T-shirt?"

"Of course not!" She pulled it off and turned once slowly so I could get the full effect of the shorts and bikini top ensemble.

"Yeah, I reckon that got his attention. He's all set then?"

Thankfully the t-shirt went back on.

"Yep! He's going to meet us at Shark's boat at six tomorrow morning. I told him we'd give him a ride, but he insisted on driving his Hummer." Consuelo did a quick eye roll. "Probably true in his case what they say about men with big fancy trucks." She held up a bent little finger.

"So, that's set. Anything else?"

"Yeah, he rambled on about his great Hummer and tried to convince me to ride with him in the morning, but he didn't try to get me to come inside the houseboat. I figure he has company tonight."

She left us with that to mull over and went back to banging things in the galley.

"Slip, you talk to Jimmy?"

"Yeah, we're all set. It should be plenty dark still when Butthole leaves in the morning. I'll go up to the boat first, see if there's a guard."

He acted like that was it. I knew better. He had a little twitch at the corner of his mouth going like he did anytime he was holding back.

"And?"

"Candygram."

He headed for the guest bedroom. Consuelo brought a platter of food out to the dining table and went back for more.

I took another sip of soup and eased over to check out the food our lovely chef had prepared. I noticed there were only two place settings as she set bowls of mashed potatoes, gravy, and green beans next to the platter of steaks and chops. She gave me a wink and turned toward the direction Slip had gone.

"Put it back in your pants and get in here before it gets cold and I have to throw it to the hogs!"

Slip came running for the table and stopped in front of me. He had on what looked like a Zorro hat and mask and held a box wrapped in fancy paper. The man had a wide-open grin on his face.

"Candygram!"

Consuelo was already sitting and wasted no time piling food onto her plate. I gave Slip's outfit a good look.

"You found that in the clothes locker?"

Slip stood there looking at me and stealing little glances at the food.

"Yeah, you wouldn't believe all the stuff in there, some of it pretty kinky. One of the previous owners must have had a lot of lively lady friends. That's where Blondie found the shorts thing she's got on."

"What's in the box?"

"Candy?"

I doubted it but let it go. Slip took off the hat and mask, sat down, and started eating. It looked like neither of them had eaten in a week, the way they went at it. Consuelo came up from a big pull of beer.

"Sorry. You need to take it easy since you're still pretty sick. There's more soup on the stove."

I still refused to sleep in the master bedroom, which was enough for Slip to decide not to as well. He'd been sleeping on some boat cushions on the floor. A little before five, the alarm on my cell phone woke me from another good night's sleep on the old yellow couch.

I lay there a minute and took stock. Other than still being weak, I felt fine. As soon as I sat up and put my feet on the floor, the guest bedroom door opened and Consuelo came out dressed in fishing clothes.

"I'll have coffee in five."

We went over everything once more while sipping coffee. Slip kept looking out the window at the dark marina.

"There's lights on at Grizzel's, and I just seen Jimmy out across the lot right where he said to look. I'd say we're ready."

A minute later we heard an engine start. I peeked out the window. "That him?"

"Yep. Looks like it's a go."

Consuelo didn't have much to say, not even any wisecracks. She looked determined.

"All right, Slip. Consuelo and I are out of here. Tell Jimmy to call me and let me know what's going on. Where we're fishing there should be decent reception for the cell phone."

Consuelo grabbed our lunch out of the fridge and headed for the door. I cut the lights behind her and left Slip in the dark houseboat.

Jimmy came out of the shadows next to the car. I whispered we were set, and he whispered the same. I asked about Slip's candy box. He said he'd given Slip a sophisticated device that when pointed at a person and activated, would cause that person to lose consciousness for several minutes. Before I could say anything, he assured me it was foolproof. So I didn't mention Slip's problems with mechanical devices, figured Jimmy knew so much, he surely knew about that.

The Hummer was already there when we pulled into the old abandoned marina.

"Taco, we got a problem."

"I see."

Grizzel was standing next to his truck, but so was another man. A man just as big as Grizzel.

"I told the bastard to come alone."

"Well, let's see what's up."

It was still dark, with just the first hint of light in the east. We parked and got out.

"Morning, Harry. You ready to do a little fishing?" I could see his mean sneer in the poor light.

"Ready to kick some ass. Then get some ass!" The sneer went to a leer when he looked over at my companion.

I had to ask, "Who's your boyfriend, Harry? I thought you were coming alone."

"Hutch here is my bodyguard. You got a problem with that?"

"I reckon not. The boat's right back in there and I'm sure he's waiting on us. Y'all go on, we got your back."

I motioned for them to go ahead down the narrow path through the weeds and pulled Consuelo close as soon as they turned.

"And what is this ass dear Grizzel is talking about?"

"He started to balk yesterday, so I told him if he won

I'd give him a hummer in his Hummer. What's the problem? I mean, you *are* going to win, aren't you?"

She gave me a quick kiss on the cheek and headed down the path.

They were still grumbling introductions and instructions when I got to the boat. Shark fired up the engine and started barking orders getting ready to cast off. Consuelo went into the cabin but shot right back out.

"Shit! I forgot the lunch cooler!" She started up the plank, then turned and looked at the bodyguard. "It's pretty heavy, I could use some help."

More grumbling but he finally followed when Shark started in about hurrying the fuck up. We had the dock lines loose and were ready to shove off when Consuelo came back alone making a big show of carrying the heavy cooler. Grizzel was asking before she even got back on board.

"Where's Hutch?"

I could see her shrug in the lights from the boat as she dragged the cooler aboard.

"He tripped over something and banged his head in the dark. Then got a call on his cell. He said to go on ahead. Said he'd be back in time to pick you up."

Grizzel didn't like this much, but Shark had us pulled away from the dock and heading down the channel as soon as Consuelo and lunch were aboard.

"Gonna be a good day for sharks! Weather's perfect and I got some of my secret chum!" The old skipper pointed to a rusty drum in the stern. Other than the chum, the boat smelled better. I realized the gang must have taken Queequeg along to wherever they were holed up while we were off with the boat.

Grizzel sat in the fighting chair on deck, smoking a big cigar with Shark at the topside controls. I helped Consuelo get the cooler stowed away in the cabin. It really wasn't heavy.

"What happened to Hutch?"

Another shrug, "Snake bit him when he went in the bushes to pee?"

"What's that on your sleeve?"

"Ketchup?"

She wiped off a few red drops with a rag and gave me a quick wink before going back into the cockpit.

As soon as we cleared the channel, Shark put the hammer down and the old wreck of a boat roared along into the dawn at a good clip. A few little pieces of rotten hull planking blew off the bow each time we hit a good wave. Being pretty sure that wasn't supposed to happen, I pointed it out to our captain. He looked over from his high perch and shrugged.

Consuelo went up top, and he yelled instructions to her for a few minutes. She came down and got tackle ready while Grizzel watched her from the big chair rubbing himself and making lewd remarks. I went up to talk to the old man.

"We going where I think we're going?"

"Yep. This time of year you can't beat the Shark Hole. Should be plenty of big 'uns for you boys to play with there." He had a wild look in his eyes. Man did love his sharks. "I done told dipstick the rules like we talked about before. First with a fish on gets the chair until it's landed. Biggest shark by noon wins."

Consuelo had the heavy poles ready by the time we got to the spot. The old man set the engine idling just enough to hold more-or-less in place against the current.

I got baited up and started in fishing off the starboard side. Grizzel sat in the big chair like he expected Consuelo to do everything for him, until Shark yelled at him to get off his fat ass and start fishing.

Consuelo went up to the helm to steer when the old man came down to start in with the chumming. Grizzel had his bait out by then off the port side, and as the captain walked by the big man gave him a hard kick in the rear. Shark went down but when he came up he had a fish club in his hands. Grizzel started laughing.

"You wouldn't dare, you old fool!"

It was still early enough the old captain hadn't put on his sunglasses, so I could see Grizzel was getting the rage version of the holding eye and roving eye thing. The laughter tapered off. It looked like the barefoot old man was about to start in with the club any second.

Consuelo yelled from up top and pointed. It broke the stare-down when they looked. Shark flashed a deranged grin at the lawyer before answering the helmswoman.

"Them's porpoise, honey, not sharks!"

I knew she knew the difference. Grizzel turned around and looked.

"Dumb bitch probably never saw a real shark!"

It wasn't long after the chum slick got going that we all saw real sharks. Several dark shapes could be seen in the clear blue water, and a couple of times fins broke the surface, some of them good sized. All the bouncing around in the boat hadn't done me a lot of good. I was trying to save my strength in case I had to deal with any sharks on my line.

The old man acted different. He stayed at the stern, doling out the exceptionally rank chum and quietly taking plenty of verbal abuse from Grizzel, who had obviously already forgotten the fish club. Once I caught the captain's eye and he gave me the smallest wink.

I snuck a look at my watch just as Grizzel hooked up and jumped in the big chair. Shark strapped him in to the chair so the pull of the fish would be on the chair as much as on the fisherman. Grizzel acted like he had a monster, but with the big reel he had it up close enough to see pretty quick. The old man looked over the side.

"Black-tip, maybe four foot."

He shrugged and looked at me just as something hit my bait hard. I braced my hip against the side of the boat, but the fish ran straight back and pulled me against the stern. It felt like something serious, and I was just trying to keep from being pulled overboard as the fish ran and line peeled out. The old man appeared next to me, ready to grab my belt. He looked back at Grizzel still in the big chair, grinning.

"Get your little fish in the boat and your fat ass out of that chair! He's got something worthwhile here!" Grizzel let the chair straps hold his pole while he lit another cigar.

"I ain't got this brute in the boat yet! Rules is rules, captain!"

Grizzel started in on a good hard laugh but stopped suddenly when Shark ran across the boat and cut Grizzel's line with the knife that had suddenly materialized in his hand.

"Hey! What the fuck!"

Shark turned toward Grizzel, still holding the knife.

"Out of the chair!"

After a round of particularly nasty curses aimed at the old captain, Grizzel finally dislodged his bulk from the chair. By then I had my fish stopped, but I had a hell of a time getting across the deck to the fighting chair. Shark strapped me in and my aching arms got a little bit of a break finally.

"What's the matter, writer-man? That little shark kicked your ass already?" I reached behind me with one arm and felt along the seat.

"This your wallet, Harry?"

My shark had started a sideways run and I let the big lawyer get close enough for a good pop on the side of his head with the rod tip. The old man grabbed him trying not to laugh.

"Careful there, Big 'Un! That big shark's making a move!"

The blow stunned Grizzel for a second but then he gave me a hard look. He started to say something, but the old man dragged him to the other side of the boat and told him to stay out of the way.

By the time my shark came to the side, I was so exhausted I was about to get sick. I snuck a look up top while they were busy measuring the fish still in the water with a long flexible pole. Consuelo had been quiet, holding the boat on course. I could see the concern on her face. I gave her a weak thumbs up just as Shark dropped the pvc measuring stick back on the deck.

"Seven-foot-three-inch bull shark! Nice one, Taco!" He produced a rusty pair of wire cutters and at last the pressure was off the rod and the shark was gone.

Grizzel started back in bitching and complaining while Shark got him re-rigged and fishing again. The secure cell phone Jimmy gave me had been vibrating off and on for several minutes. The first time a good ten minutes before the agreed upon call times. I managed to get to a bunk in the cabin while Grizzel took the chair again and laughed at me. I could hear Consuelo then, yelling at the old man to relieve her.

The next time the phone went off I had it.

"That you?"

"Yeah, thought you were out of range or something."

"I had my hands full, what you got?"

"We're in, been in for a while. Slip's standing lookout."

Consuelo came into the cabin at a run, "Are you —"

I held my hand over the phone. "They're in." I went back to Jimmy. "No problems then? No one else there?"

"Oh, there was someone else here."

"So Slip used the device you gave him?"

"No. He said he was having problems with it so he put something else in the candybox."

"What?"

"A brick. Guy opened the door and Slip yells, 'Candygram' at the top of his lungs and starts smashing the guy in the face with the box. Guy's still out, lying on the floor."

"Who is it?"

"One of the Blue Manatee thugs, I guess. Some big guy with a white X on his face."

"Well, you should have at least another hour or two. Our boy is well occupied." Out on deck I could hear Grizzel yelling at the captain again. "You finding what you're looking for?"

"I just got in what looks like his main computer files, and we've already got a lot of paper files, tapes, and pictures. If I can't find what I'm looking for soon, we'll take the computers too. I'd just like to know for sure that what we need is here."

"Good luck. I'll let you know if anything changes on my end."

"Right, same here."

I punched the phone off and dropped it on the bunk. Consuelo had a cool, wet cloth for my forehead and a warm smile for the rest of me.

"Taco, how much longer do we have to baby-sit this moron? We don't take him back soon, I think either Shark or myself are going to be doing some dental work on him with that fish billy."

"I know. As soon as we get word from Jimmy that he has what he's looking for, we'll head in."

I saw those bright blue eyes soften above me. I knew what was coming and tried to raise a hand to stop the pair of slowly incoming lips. But there was a strong hand holding down each of mine. I was too weak to resist and relaxed on the bunk. I could feel her sweet breath on my face and her body began to press against me just as Grizzel's reel and Grizzel both started screaming like banshees.

"AHHH!!! I got you now, motherfucker!"

We ran back to the cockpit just as the old skipper finished strapping Grizzel and the big rod to the seat. Consuelo went up top to get the boat back on course while Shark yelled instructions to her and Grizzel. Line was still peeling off the big reel. Then the fish jumped, about three hundred yards straight back. A big one. The old shark fisherman took his hat off and held it reverently over his heart.

"Mako. Biggest I seen in years. Go twelve feet at least."

He turned slowly to look at the big sweaty man straining in the fighting chair. He shook his head and spit, obviously disgusted Grizzel would hook into so fine a specimen.

The shark sounded and after a few minutes the lawyer relaxed and let the seat straps do most of the work. The shark came up again and thrashed the surface. Grizzel had let the line go slack and the old man was livid.

"Reel in the slack you silly bastard! He makes another run like that first one he'll snap the line!"

Luck was on Grizzel's side, since the big mako instead sounded again and started putting slow, steady pressure on the heavy line. Grizzel lit another cigar, took a puff, then yelled up at Consuelo.

"Hey, Sugarpuss, what's this remind you of?" He worked the cigar in and out of his mouth a few times, then motioned me over. When I got close he grabbed my shirt collar and pulled my face up to his.

"Soon as I get this bad boy up to gaff, there won't be any more doubt who the best man is."

This guy was in serious need of a breath mint, but I felt the advice would go unheeded, so instead when he let loose of my shirt and popped his cigar back in his mouth and started to suck, I hit the hot end with the palm of my hand. Hard.

I got burned a little, but it was worth it to see such a big man trying so hard to grab me while strapped in and coughing up bits of cigar. Priceless.

"You fucker! That was a twenty-dollar Monte Cristo!"

Our captain brought out his first real grin of the day.

"You better pay attention, fat boy, that big fish ain't done yet!"

And it wasn't. The mako was heading deep still, but heading for the boat. If it got close enough, the line could catch the boat, rub, and break. Consuelo caught the captain's signal and moved the boat forward enough to keep the big shark behind us.

Everyone was fixed on the shark, so I saw it first. Out on the horizon, a boat as big as a cruise ship. But as it came closer over the next few minutes I could see it was jet black, stem to stern. Then Grizzel saw it.

"Ha! There she is!"

He had another cigar going by now, using it to point and yelling up at the helm. "Hey, Sweetcakes! Maybe after you get your tonsils polished tonight I'll introduce you to my boss!" He seemed to think this way funny. "You ever met a dead man?"

While the rest of the crew did their best to ignore the annoying blowhard, I slipped back in the cabin to take a call.

"You find anything?"

"I got the mother lode. He's been doing wire taps on his own clients. I guess sort of insurance. They told JB they wanted to talk about funding a children's home in the Keys, invited him out on a big boat, then threw him overboard. I just found everything, including names and phone conversations for that second Marty hit. It also looks like that county commissioner killed in a car crash a few weeks ago wasn't an accident." He hesitated for a few seconds. "Found a list of other people they planned the same treatment for. The last and newest name on the list was yours."

"I guess that's not much of a surprise, but I could have gone without hearing it all the same." My hands were shaking. I couldn't tell if it was nerves or the fever coming back again. "You about wrapped up there?"

"Yeah, I'm transferring a bunch of files to DC now so they can see some of what I've got. We're going to finish loading everything in ice chests next and stroll out of here."

"Sounds good. I'm sure you'll be in touch."

"You bet, and thanks for your help. I thank you and your country thanks you."

"I'll pass that last part along to our host when we get in." I almost punched off, then remembered. "There's a really big black boat out here our boy seems awful fond of. Know anything about that?"

"If it's the Big Black Boat, then there's likely someone on board we'd like to have a word with. I'll pass that along as soon as I can."

"Later, then."

"Later."

Back on deck Grizzel was more excited about the black boat than the several hundred pounds of prehistoric eating machine he had on the end of his line. He was horsing the fish in fast now, ignoring the forty years of shark-fishing experience being yelled in his ear.

"He ain't near tired yet! You been dicking around, letting him rest instead of working him! Let him make a couple more long runs before you get him up here by the boat!"

Grizzel pulled the fish up by the port side of the old boat and started jerking hard on the rod like he expected to yank aboard hundreds of pounds of the ocean's deadliest creature.

"Get over there and pull him in, old man!"

"I ain't getting near him yet! I told you —"

The giant shark came easy until he bumped the side of the boat, then water and pieces of boat exploded into the air and the shark made a hard run straight back. Grizzel was holding on for all he was worth with the reel screaming out line again. Clarence "Shark" Hunter walked over to the straining lawyer and got up in his face, smiling.

"Now do you believe me?"

Grizzel turned red in the face and spit hard in the old man's face.

"You old bag of shit! I get this fish in I just might throw you overboard like we did that faggy manatee!"

Shark took a couple of slow steps to the side of Grizzel, still smiling, with spit running down his cheek.

"That so, big boy? You going to hurt me, are you?"

The mako had been slowing a little but started another hard run then, putting a terrific strain on Grizzel, the rod and reel, and the seat. Grizzel started in yelling curses at the old man over the noise of the reel. Shark stepped closer to the sweaty lawyer and gave him a quick kiss on the cheek. Grizzel looked over, shocked.

"Huh?"

Shark never took his eyes from those of the perplexed lawyer while he hooked his big toe in the ring on the pin in the seat pedestal. There was a metallic "ping" as the pin came out, followed by a short scream, a wet thud, and a big splash behind the boat. The old man took a bucket of water and washed his face, then the two bloody marks Grizzel's knees had left on the stern on his way to join the big shark. I just stood there staring at the place where the fighting chair had been. Between the weight of the chair

and the pull of the shark, Harry Grizzel had sunk like a
rock.

Consuelo cut the engines and jumped down to the
deck. She walked to the back of the boat, waved goodbye,
and yelled into the distance.

"So I guess tonight's off, Harry?" When there was no
answer she turned to me and shrugged. "Looks like I'm
free this evening. Got any plans?"

Chapter Twenty-Three

It came to me on the way in why the old shark fisherman had insisted I use the newer heavy rod and reel. But mostly my mind just ran the scene of Grizzel and chair going over the stern of the boat.

Back at the dock we inspected the damage the big shark had done to the side of the boat. It looked pretty serious. If Shark hadn't rigged an extra bilge pump on the way back in, we might not have made it. He didn't seem too concerned though.

"No problem. I got forty years' experience patching up old boats and several wired young partners who need something to do to work off a little nervous energy before tonight anyway."

I was exhausted by the time we got back to my place later that afternoon. Jimmy called and said the haul from Grizzel's was even better than he'd thought earlier. I told him I didn't think Grizzel would be around for a while.

When I told him what happened, he thought about it for a minute then said he'd write it up as Grizzel last seen leaving his houseboat early that morning. We never did see the bodyguard or the Hummer again.

Jimmy had slipped some cash expense money to Slip on some pretense, but I felt too poorly still to go out with him and Consuelo that evening. Turns out Floaters was up, open and having a special on stone crab claws. But as luck would have it, the restaurant had sunk again the next day when Slip and I rolled up in my truck.

"Well, poo. Really, Taco, it was open last night."

"So much for that. Governor's?"

I was feeling mighty good driving my old truck to the restaurant for an early lunch. Knowing I had done my part to help my country and community, that and ten hours of sound sleep, had me feeling like a new man.

Slip was wired, about to blow, just dying to tell me all the goings-on of the night before. Consuelo had to work a shift at the hotel, and it was strange not having her around. She said her sisters were on her bad about taking so much time off.

We got to Governor's just as they opened. Since the place was nearly empty, we were able to get a table in back with some privacy. I was hungry as a bear, but took my time with the menu. I contemplated the Eighteen Wheeler while Slip started filling me in.

"You hear about that fancy Blue Manatee Park?"

"No, what happened? Someone writing on the signs again?"

"Nah, better than that. While you were off fishing on Shark Hunter's boat, some politicians and Blue Manatee big shots were giving speeches for TV cameras. About the time they got going good, some kind of mutant skunk-dog ran up on the stage and bit the shit out of a couple of 'em and scared hell out of the rest. The perp run off, but from what I heard from folks and seen in the paper this morning, it sounds like it might have been that aromatic set of walking teeth Shark calls a dog."

"Wouldn't surprise me."

"Anyway, since Blondie had gone on home last night, I was planning on taking the guest room. You were dead to the world on that old couch, but I was still wired about the little game me and Jimmy run on Grizzel's place. So I figured I'd head over to the other side of the island, see if there might be any mischief needed doing around that fancy new park or the construction site."

The Offroad looked good, but I didn't really feel like a salad.

"I stopped on the way and had a few beers so I wouldn't be getting thirsty in the middle of anything. Just as I walked out of the bar, here comes a big explosion from the direction of the new development."

The waitress came and I decided on the Skidmark — bacon strips on a chicken patty — with a side of Road Gravel. Slip ordered a complicated array of foods without opening the menu. The waitress left.

"So I ran over a few blocks to take a look and ended up sneaking out on that causeway they'd just built. With everything that was happening out on the water by then, the guards weren't paying much attention to anything else. At one point they all got in a truck and hauled ass, so I looked around and found a big bulldozer with the key in it and pushed a few Blue Manatee pickups, a backhoe, and some other stuff in the water." He took a quick conspiratorial glance around. "You know, I thought with big ol' tires full of air like that, those loaders might float some, but they don't float a bit."

We got our drinks and each took a long pull.

"So then, here comes some of the guards back, all worked up about their headquarters being all smashed and on fire."

"How did that happen?"

"Beats me. I did run into the building a few times with the dozer, but damned if I know how it caught on fire." He gave me a blameless shrug.

"So what happened out on the water? Was that Shark Hunter and those folks?"

"Yeah, at least at first it was. After those guards came back and started running around like a bunch of ants and yelling into their radios, I jumped into their truck they'd been nice enough to leave running. There were plenty of other folks out there gawking by then, so as I left the scene I kinda scrunched down so nobody would see me in case it turned out later my actions might be seen as some sort of infractions of the law." A sly smile.

"It was real late, but I headed for the Scorpion Pit, since I knew that's where Shark and his gang would likely be stopping for refreshments after an evening of mayhem. The place was closed by then, so I parked the truck in the middle of the empty parking lot and climbed up in a tree next to the building. About the time I got settled in good, here comes that little car of Julie's barreling into the parking lot at a hard slide right into the truck. Smashed shit out of both vehicles, but Julie and the rest of 'em jump out laughing like it's the funniest thing ever. They break into the bar and go right up to Shark's usual table and start partying like a bunch of pirates coming ashore, which I guess is about right.

"Anyway, they're all sitting around drinking and talking about the evening's excitement. All I got to do is listen in and not fall out of the tree. Seems Shark knows some old fella who's always going out with his boat looking for stuff after a storm. A few years back the fella found one of the old mines the Navy put out for German subs during the war. They traded a case of liquor and Shark's ex-wife Levita for the mine, and that newspaper fella figured out just where to put it. So they got the mine set in the right place with a GPS, then eased over in the dark and hooked up one of those giant sand barges they anchor over by the construction site every night. Towed it over real sneaky-like, cut it loose, and watched the tide take it right into the mine. That was the big explosion I heard."

The food arrived and I started while Slip tried to talk faster so he could jump in himself.

"The gang sat there drinking and had a lot of nice stuff to say about how things built with American engineering, especially mines, are built to last. I guess that old mine blew the shit out of the giant barge and sunk it dead in the middle of the main shipping channel. Totally blocked the channel so there ain't going to be any sand barges coming through there for a while."

Slip inhaled a few of what looked like real small barbeque ribs, then went back to his report.

"When the mine blew, they all started whooping and hollering out there on Shark's old boat thinking that was it, but it wasn't. Not by a long shot.

"Shark said it was like flipping on the kitchen light and seeing roaches scatter. The mine blowing like that lit up the whole area for a few seconds. Until then they didn't know that less than a mile away was a black cruise ship with no lights and several other dark boats that looked like they were creeping up on it. As soon as the mine blew the little boats and the big one started shooting at each other with all kinds of machine guns and rockets and shit. That's what me, the Blue Manatee guards, and a bunch of other people were seeing from land. Looked like the Fourth of July going on with all those little boats chasing the big one hauling ass and all shooting at each other. That went on for an hour or so. The big one and at least one of the little ones were on fire by the time they got out of sight."

"That's some story. I take it Shark and his crew are all okay."

"Levita wasn't there, I think being part of the trade for the mine was her idea. But the rest were all fit and frisky last I saw, getting drunk as skunks." Which reminded Slip to drain his beer and motion to the waitress for another. He gave me a wink. "That Julie sounds mighty sweet on you. Kept asking old Shark about you and hanging on his every word. Not a bad-looking gal in that lingerie and ammo belt outfit. You don't know if she ever taught any school, do you?"

I noticed a flurry of mischievous winks going on across the table. "I'll ask when I see her next. So did you?" I held a spoonful of rice and peas over my plate in a questioning way.

"Did I what?" I knew he knew what I was asking.

"You know ...," I let the food fall off my spoon.

"If you must know, yes, I fell out of the damn tree. Sprained my ankle some, but it loosened back up when I was running from the gang. Luckily they were all pretty well potted by then and none of 'em very good shots."

The waitress brought a couple more Coronas.

"Jimmy says that little trick you and him pulled on Grizzel went just fine."

"Yeah, I can't wait to see the look on Grizzel's face."

I was getting a sideways glance from my tablemate.

"Actually, I ain't seen your neighbor since y'all went fishing yesterday. How'd that work out?"

"I pretty much won by default. I think the strain of the competition might have been a little much for Grizzel. He may have gone on holiday for a while to relax."

The sideways look continued.

"Yeah, that's kinda what Consuelo said. She also said to give you this. I guess for you to put your keys on."

He dropped a stainless steel pin and ring on the table.

I called Consuelo as soon as we got back to the marina. Slip went off to see someone he was supposed to help do some work on their boat.

"I got the pin you gave Slip."

"Don't worry, I didn't say anything to him. I just thought you might like a little memento."

"Not really, but thanks anyway. I wanted to tell you I'm feeling a lot better and about to take a nap — on the bed in the master stateroom."

"I'm the only one here at the hotel. Wait, maybe I can get the guy across the street to cover for me. I'll be there in fifteen minutes, maybe ten."

"That's not what I meant. I know why I couldn't sleep right."

I told her about the fever dream I had and had just remembered the night before. When she cleaned and rearranged the houseboat she'd hidden the weird little gold statues, the chacmools, in the bedroom. I told her I didn't know why, but I was pretty sure those had been causing the bad nightmares. She said she had to go because a busload of tourists had pulled up in front and most of its contents were spilling into the hotel. I told her I'd talk to her later and called Jimmy.

Jimmy didn't answer the phone. Ten minutes later he came aboard my houseboat. He looked worried.

"You better not call me for a while, things have taken a turn."

I told him to take a load off and we both had a seat in the lounge.

"My employers weren't too interested in the information I came up with until I mentioned a possible sighting of the big boat." He nodded toward me. "Not long after that some guys from another department showed up and hauled off everything I had, including my own computer."

"That sucks."

He shrugged and took a clear plastic package of small silver discs out of his shoe. "Always do a back-up, my friend." He grinned and the discs went back. "I'll start feeding your buddy Shawn some tasty bits of information. Between that and the little party out past the reef last night, I don't think we have to worry about Blue Manatee anymore."

"Well, that's good to hear. Seen in the paper the navy claims all that action on the water last night was just routine maneuvers."

He just smiled a little and winked. Guess I wasn't going to find out what happened to the Big Black Boat.

"What about those murders? The two Marty Manatees and the commissioner?" He tapped his foot.

"Shawn's going to be a busy newspaperman for quite a while. I wouldn't be surprised if when it's all over, there aren't people lined up to give him journalism awards and book contracts."

I gave him the cell phone and other goodies he'd lent me. After he left I stretched out on the trusty old couch for some serious contemplating.

After that good night's sleep, a mighty fine feed at Gov's, and another reminder from Jimmy that I'd done good for my country, I felt like I had all of life's bases covered. Except one.

I reached over and made a call, then took a pleasant, dream-free nap.

Chapter Twenty-Four

I'd just gotten showered and dressed when Slip came by, all full of nervous energy.

"Hey, TB, you still feeling okay?"

"Never better. What's up?"

I checked my watch and started tidying up the lounge.

"Oh, nothing. I just need to use your phone a minute, make a quick call."

"Problem?"

"No, no problem, not really. I just wanted to call Lefty, see if him and some of the boys over at the fire station could stop by Capt. Roy's in the next few minutes."

I tossed him the phone and started the vacuum cleaner. He made his call outside, then ran off.

Later that evening, there was a soft knock at my door.

"Julie, come on in."

"Hey, Taco Bob."

She was dressed different — a short black dress and heels, her long dark hair shining. I directed her toward the couch.

"Shawn got an anonymous e-mail this afternoon. Very detailed information on my brother's murder. He got in touch with the police, and it looks like they should have a case. There was some other stuff about Blue Manatee as well. With the construction already stopped, it looks like they're out of business around here." She slid closer to me on the couch. "I don't know how I could ever repay you for all you did." She put a warm hand on my bare leg. I checked to make sure my robe was presentable.

"Hey, glad to help. Sounds like you did your fair share as well." I looked at the clock on the wall. "I'd offer you something, but it's kind of late."

"No thanks, I'm fine."

"So, how are you and Shawn getting along these days?" The hand on my leg jumped and the dreamy look in her eyes changed. "He seems a good fella, hard worker."

"Uh, yes, he is." She fiddled with the hem of her dress, then stuck her chin out a little. "In fact, that's what I was going to tell you. He got his old job back with the Key West paper, and we're getting a place together. A real nice place, actually, just a couple of blocks off Truman. You'll have to stop by sometime."

"I'll do her! It's nice to see everything work out for you." Though she didn't look too happy at the moment.

"Yeah, thanks. I should go."

I gave her a quick hug at the door and escorted her to the dock so she didn't have an accident with those high heels in the dark.

As soon as I came back in and closed the door, the phone rang.

"Hello?"

"Hey, it's me. What's shaking?"

"Not much, Consuelo."

"Just thought I'd check on you, see how you felt."

"I'm right as rain, but thanks for asking."

"Well, if you need anything, I could come over. My sisters all ran off somewhere again, but Slip's here. I think he's hiding from someone. He can keep an eye on things if you need me to bring you anything."

"No, I think I got everything I need. Maybe if you're free tomorrow afternoon, we can talk Slip into going fishing on the Wilbur for a few hours."

"Okay, I gotta go. Capt. Roy just came in."

I unplugged the phone and made myself a drink and one for the lady. She lay stretched out facing me on the big bed in the master bedroom, a towel modestly over her rear. She turned a page of my manuscript and took a sip of her drink before asking.

"Well?"

"Sorry about that. It doesn't rain, but it pours."

I sat on the edge of the bed, pulled the towel away, and took a leisurely gaze at some pleasant bare curves. "Lady, you do have a lovely back."

"Oh, bloody right! I bet you say that back line to all the birds who flock around here!" She laughed and rolled over, dropping her mop of blue hair in my lap. She took my hands and placed them on her breasts. "But don't you know, there's two sides to Everything, eh?"

She dropped the little doll inside the headboard drawer where the Chacmools had been and switched off the light.

GULF OF MEXICO

Key West

Sugarloaf Key

Stock Island

Boca Chica

Key Manatee

Pine Island

Seven Mile
Bridge

Bahia Honda

Marathon

FLORIDA KEYS

Acknowledgments

I would like to thank everyone who has read my previous books for the kind words and encouragement, especially bestselling writers Christopher Moore and Randy Wayne White.

Thanks also to Sara Leigh, Barbara, Eva, and Bob, as well as Jeff, Scott, Deb, and the rest of the folks from the CM board who helped put together what is now *Key Manatee.*

Besides the book you hold in your hands, Robert Tacoma is the author of *Key Weird, Key Weirder,* and *Key Witch.* He lives in central Florida and is always writing another book.